A Christmas Carol

小氣財神

Original Author   Charles Dickens
Adaptor   Scott Fisher
Illustrator   Ludmila Pipchenko

WORDS
600

MP3

Let's Enjoy Masterpieces!

All the beautiful fairy tales and masterpieces that you have encountered during your childhood remain as warm memories in your adulthood. This time, let's indulge in the world of masterpieces through English. You can enjoy the depth and beauty of original works, which you can't enjoy through Chinese translations.

The stories are easy for you to understand because of your familiarity with them. When you enjoy reading, your ability to understand English will also rapidly improve.

This series of **Let's Enjoy Masterpieces** is a special reading comprehension booster program, devised to improve reading comprehension for beginners whose command of English is not satisfactory, or who are elementary, middle, and high school students. With this program, you can enjoy reading masterpieces in English with fun and efficiency.

This carefully planned program is composed of 5 levels, from the beginner level of 350 words to the intermediate and advanced levels of 1,000 words. With this program's level-by-level system, you are able to read famous texts in English and to savor the true pleasure of the world's language.

The program is well conceived, composed of reader-friendly explanations of English expressions and grammar, quizzes to help the student learn vocabulary and understand the meaning of the texts, and fabulous illustrations that adorn every page. In addition, with our "Guide to Listening," not only is reading comprehension enhanced but also listening comprehension skills are highlighted.

In the audio recording of the book, texts are vividly read by professional American actors. The texts are rewritten, according to the levels of the readers by an expert editorial staff of native speakers, on the basis of standard American English with the ministry of education recommended vocabulary. Therefore, it will be of great help even for all the students that want to learn English.

Please indulge yourself in the fun of reading and listening to English through *Let's Enjoy Masterpieces*.

狄更斯

Charles Dickens
(1812-1870)

Charles Dickens was a great English novelist. He couldn't receive an appropriate school education in his childhood because he was born to a poor family. He began to work in a factory at the age of 12. In the early 19th century, British capitalism began to flourish, bringing prosperity to big cities in England. However, there were also dark sides to capitalism. Child labor thrived, and the working class suffered from great poverty.

With an insight born from his own bitter experiences with social injustice, Charles Dickens began to write short stories in order to educate himself. He was determined that his quest for self-education would pull him out of poverty.

Dickens' novels are highly respected for vivid descriptions of the daily life of working-class people. He knew from his own experience their joys and sorrows. Dickens' brave and humorous portrayals also examined injustice and social contradictions.

His best-known works include *Great Expectations* and *Oliver Twist*. He was often criticized for trying to appeal to the sentimental and melodramatic tastes of his readers. But the reason that Dickens, along with Shakespeare, is held in high regard as a great English novelist is that he created characters full of humanity and humor. These characters exhibit the faults, resilience, and vitality of real human beings.

On June 9th, 1870, Charles Dickens died. His death was mourned by the entire world, and he was laid to rest in Westminster Abbey, alongside England's other great writers.

Written in 1843, **A Christmas Carol** is the timeless tale of the mean miser named Scrooge. He is a mean-spirited, miserly old man. Scrooge views Christmas as nothing but a ridiculous money-wasting scheme. Then, he sees the ghost of Jacob Marley, his deceased business partner. Jacob informs Scrooge that three spirits will visit him on Christmas Eve.

Sure enough, on Christmas Eve, Scrooge receives separate visits from the ghosts of Christmas Past, Present, and Future. The three ghosts show Scrooge the errors of his ways by showing him the past, present, and future.

The ghost of Christmas Past allows Scrooge to see his gradual decline from innocent boyhood to his adult life as a miserable miser. The ghost of Christmas Present shows Scrooge the happy lives of his poor employee and nephew. Scrooge's own grave is where the ghost of Christmas Future takes him in order to learn of how he will die a lonely death. Scrooge sees the miserable end to his greedy and self-serving life.

Thanks to the three ghosts, when Scrooge wakes up on Christmas morning, he has been transformed. He changes his life and becomes a generous, kind-hearted soul.

A Christmas Carol, adapted for children, is read and loved around the world. It teaches you about finding true happiness in your life. *A Christmas Carol* is a famous book that created a new literary genre within the Christmas story.

HOW TO USE THIS BOOK
本書使用說明

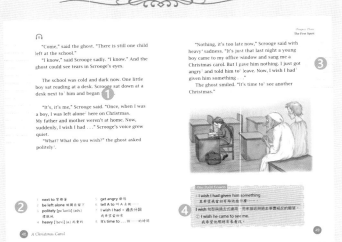

1. Original English texts

It is easy to understand the meaning of the text, because the text is rewritten according to the levels of the readers.

2. Explanation of the vocabulary

The words and expressions that include vocabulary above the elementary level are clearly defined.

3. Response notes

Spaces are included in the book so you can take notes about what you don't understand or what you want to remember.

4. One point lesson

In-depth analyses of major grammar points and expressions help you to understand sentences with difficult grammar.

∩ Audio Recording

In the audio recording, native speakers narrate the texts in standard American English. By combining the written words and the audio recording, you can listen to English with great ease.

Audio books have been popular in Britain and America for many decades. They allow the listener to experience the proper word pronunciation and sentence intonation that add important meaning and drama to spoken English. Students will benefit from listening to the recording twenty or more times.

After you are familiar with the text and recording, listen once more with your eyes closed to check your listening comprehension. Finally, after you can listen with your eyes closed and understand every word and every sentence, you are then ready to mimic the native speaker.

Then you should make a recording by reading the text yourself. Then play both recordings to compare your oral skills with those of a native speaker.

HOW TO IMPROVE
READING ABILITY
如何增進英文閱讀能力

① *Catch key words*

Read the key words in the sentences and practice catching the gist of the meaning of the sentence. You might question how working with a few important words could enhance your reading ability. However, it's quite effective. If you continue to use this method, you will find out that the key words and your knowledge of people and situations enables you to understand the sentence.

② *Divide long sentences*

Read in chunks of meaning, dividing sentences into meaningful chunks of information. In the book, chunks are arranged in sentences according to meaning. If you consider the sentences backwards or grammatically, your reading speed will be slow and you will find it difficult to listen to English.

You are ready to move to a more sophisticated level of comprehension when you find that narrowly focusing on chunks is irritating. Instead of considering the chunks, you will make it a habit to read the sentence from the beginning to the end to figure out the meaning of the whole.

❸ Make inferences and assumptions

Making inferences and assumptions is part of your ability. If you don't know, try to guess the meaning of the words. Although you don't know all the words in context, don't go straight to the dictionary. Developing an ability to make inferences in the context is important.

The first way to figure out the meaning of a word is from its context. If you cannot make head or tail out of the meaning of a word, look at what comes before or after it. Ask yourself what can happen in such a situation. Make your best guess as to the word's meaning. Then check the explanations of the word in the book or look up the word in a dictionary.

❹ Read a lot and reread the same book many times

There is no shortcut to mastering English. Only if you do a lot of reading will you make your way to the summit. Read fun and easy books with an average of less than one new word per page. Try to immerse yourself in English as often as you can.

Spend time "swimming" in English. Language learning research has shown that immersing yourself in English will help you improve your English, even though you may not be aware of what you're learning.

CONTENTS

Before You Read

Scrooge

My name is Ebenezer Scrooge. I hate to spend money or give money away. I have only one thing to say about Christmas: "Bah, humbug!"

Marley

I am Jacob Marley. I used to be partners with Ebenzer Scrooge. Unfortunately, I died seven years ago. Now, I must wear a chain and walk through the world of the living.

Bob Crachit

I am Bob Crachit. I work for Mr. Scrooge as a clerk. I have a beautiful family and a good life. I work very hard, but sadly I don't make much money.

Fred

My name is Fred. I am Mr. Scrooge's nephew. I am quite different from my uncle. I like to laugh and spend time with my lovely family. I guess I take after my mother.

Christmas Ghost of Past

I am the Ghost of Christmas Past. I show Ebenezer Scrooge his past Christmases. I try to make him see his faults by reminding him of better times.

Christmas Ghost of Present

I am the Ghost of Christmas Present. I show Ebenezer Scrooge scenes from this Christmas, which will hopefully convince him to change his miserly ways.

Christmas Ghost of Future

I am the Ghost of Christmas Future. I must show Ebenezer Scrooge what waits for him in the future if he remains a heartless, mean old man.

Chapter One

Scrooge

A long, long time ago, Scrooge and Marley had been good business partners.[1] Each had tried to work harder than the other. Each had wanted to be richer than the other.

Even now, seven years after Marley had died, the company was still called[2] 'Scrooge and Marley.' If you went to their office, that is what you would see on the door, 'Scrooge and Marley.' But now the only owner[3] was Scrooge.

1. **business partner** 生意夥伴
2. **be called** 被稱為
3. **owner** [`ounər] (n.) 所有人
4. **mean** [mi:n] (a.)
   小氣的；心地不好的
5. **miserly** [`maɪzərli] (a.)
   吝嗇的；貪婪的
6. **cold** [kould] (a.) 冷酷的
7. **hate (V-ing/to do)**
   [heɪt] (v.) 討厭做……
8. **give away** 贈送；分發
9. **tiny** [`taɪni] (a.)
   極小的；微小的
10. **weak** [wi:k] (a.) 衰弱的
11. **brittle** [`brɪtl] (a.)
   冷淡的；無人味的
12. **charcoal** [`tʃɑːrkoul] (n.) 木炭

Scrooge was known by everyone to be mean[4], miserly[5], and cold[6]. He hated[7] spending money and he hated giving money away[8] even more. And cold? Scrooge's thin white lips, icy blue nose, and tiny[9] red eyes showed the cold.

His weak[10], brittle[11] voice could make you hear the cold. Feeling the cold was the worst —he kept his office very, very cold, especially at Christmas. He hated to buy charcoal[12] for the fire, so his office was always cold and dark.

One Point Lesson

● Each **had tried** to work harder than the other.
每個人都試著比別人更努力工作。

---

had + 過去分詞 (past participle)：過去完成式，用來說明過去已經發生的事件。

● I **had lived** in Tainan before I moved to Taipei two years ago.
兩年前我搬到台北之前，一直住在台南。

15

Though[1] it was only three o'clock in the afternoon, it was already getting dark because of the heavy[2], wet fog. The only other person in the office was Bob Cratchit, Scrooge's clerk[3]. Bob was sitting next to a tiny fire. He tried warming[4] his hands over the candle he was using for light, but that couldn't help.

1. **though** [ðoʊ] (conj.)
   雖然；儘管
2. **heavy** [ˋhevi] (a.)
   多的；大量的
3. **clerk** [klɜːk] (n.) 文書職員
4. **warm** [wɔːrm] (v.) 使暖和
5. **merry** [ˋmeri] (a.)
   快樂的；歡欣的

"Merry[5] Christmas, Uncle!" a cheerful[6] voice suddenly said. It was Scrooge's young nephew[7], Fred.

"Bah[8], humbug[9]," answered Scrooge. He looked angry about having his work interrupted[10].

"Humbug! Why do you think Christmas is a humbug, Uncle?" Fred looked warm. "Surely[11] you don't mean that[12]. Everyone likes Christmas."

"Yes, I do mean it," said Scrooge. "Merry Christmas, what is there to be merry about? Aren't you poor? You have nothing to be happy about."

"Well, why aren't you happy, Uncle? You are very rich," Fred answered with a smile.

6. **cheerful** [`tʃɪrfl] (a.)
   快樂的；興高采烈的
7. **nephew** [`nefjuː] (n.)
   姪子；外甥
8. **bah** [bɑː] (int.)
   呸；哼（表示輕蔑或厭惡）
9. **humbug** [`hʌmbʌg] (n.)
   胡說八道；騙人的話

10. **interrupt** [ɪntə`rʌpt] (v.)
    打斷；阻礙
11. **surely** [`ʃurli] (adv.)
    一定地；當然地
12. **do not mean that**
    沒有那個意思

Scrooge was getting angry[1]. "There are many fools in the world wishing[2] each other[3] 'Merry Christmas' when they don't even have any money!"

"Uncle, please! It's such a nice time of year."

"Nice? What is nice? I never make any money[4] on Christmas because no one ever works." Scrooge didn't understand Christmas.

"But Christmas isn't about money, Uncle." said Fred. "I love Christmas. It's a time to be happy and generous[5]!"

1. **get angry** 被激怒
2. **wish** [wɪʃ] (v.) 祝福；但願
3. **each other** 彼此；互相
4. **make money** 賺錢
5. **generous** [ˋdʒenərəs] (a.) 慷慨的；心胸寬大的

Bob, in his tiny office, agreed. "You are right, sir. Merry Christmas to you."

"You get back to [6] work," Scrooge ordered [7]. "Or you won't have a job to be merry about."

"Don't be angry, Uncle. I just came to invite [8] you to Christmas dinner." Fred knew his uncle didn't like Christmas, but he felt sorry for Scrooge. Scrooge had no family.

"No, I'm too busy. You have your Christmas, and I'll have mine. Now leave me alone [9]."

6. **get back to** 回到……
7. **order** [`ɔːrdər] (v.) 命令
8. **invite** [ɪn`vaɪt] (v.) 邀請
9. **leave alone** 避免打擾

"But won't you join[1] us, Uncle? We are family, and we should be friends."

"Bye," was Scrooge's only answer.

"Well, I'm sorry to[2] hear that. But I wish you a merry Christmas all the same[3]."

As Fred walked out[4], he said, "Merry Christmas!" to poor[5] Bob in his cold office.

"Yes, a happy Christmas to you, too," Bob answered warmly. Then he opened the door for Fred and watched him walking away into the fog.

"Two poor fools wishing each other a merry Christmas," Scrooge said.

1. **join** [dʒɔɪn] (v.) 加入；參與
2. **sorry to** 對……感到遺憾
3. **all the same** 依然；還是
4. **walk out** 走出去
5. **poor** [pʊr] (a.) 可憐的
6. **just then** 正在那時
7. **wear** [wer] (v.) 穿著
8. **interruption** [ɪntəˋrʌpʃən] (n.) 打斷；妨礙
9. **blessed** [ˋblɛsɪd] (a.) 神聖的；受祝福的
10. **ask** [æsk] (v.) 詢問；要求

Just then[6] two fat gentlemen wearing[7] expensive clothes came into the office.

"Excuse us, is this 'Scrooge and Marley's office'?"

"Yes, it is," answered Scrooge, again looking angry about an interruption[8].

"May I ask, are you Mr. Scrooge or Mr. Marley?" one of the men asked.

"Mr. Marley is dead. He died on Christmas Eve seven years ago, in 1836."

"Oh, I'm sorry," said the same man. "But we are here, at this blessed[9] time of year, to ask[10] if you would like to give some money to the poor. So many people have nothing to eat."

One Point Lesson

◆ But we are here, at this blessed time of year, to ask if you would like to give some money to **the poor**.
但是我們在這兒，在這個一年中最神聖的日子，問問您是否願意捐一些錢出來幫助窮人。

「**the + 形容詞**」：指某類的全體成員，若當作主詞，後面需加複數動詞。

e.g. **the poor** 窮人　　　　　**the rich** 富人
　　the living 活著的人　　**the dead** 死去的人

"Aren't there any prisons[1]?" asked Scrooge. "Or any orphanages[2]?"

"Well, yes, sir, there are still many prisons and orphanages."

"What about[3] poorhouses[4] for the poor?" Scrooge said with a mean look[5].

"It's sad, but there are still many poorhouses, orphanages, and prisons," said the same man. "But many people can't go there. They are cold and have little to eat. Could you please help them by donating[6] some money?"

1. **prison** [ˋprɪzən] (n.) 監獄
2. **orphanage** [ˋɔːrfənɪdʒ] (n.) 孤兒院
3. **What about . . . ?** 如何？（詢問意見或消息）
4. **poorhouse** [ˋpurhaus] (n.) 救濟院；貧民院
5. **look** [luk] (n.) 表情
6. **donate** [ˋdouneɪt] (v.) 捐助

7. **too. . . to. . .** 太……以致無法……
8. **tax** [tæks] (n.) 稅
9. **besides** [bɪˋsaɪdz] (adv.) 此外；而且
10. **tell** [tel] (v.) 發現；分辨
11. **sorrowful** [ˋsɑːroufəl] (a.) 悲傷的；憂愁的

Chapter One
Scrooge

"No, I will give no money to people who are too lazy to[7] work." said Scrooge.

"But sir, some of them could die. Won't you help them?"

"I do help them. They already get too much money from me and my taxes[8]. Besides[9], there are too many people in the world now. A few lazy fools dying is a good thing!"

The two men could tell[10] Scrooge would never give them anything. They gave Bob a sorrowful[11] look.

"Now get back to work and no more interruptions!" Scrooge shouted at his clerk.

The afternoon slowly became night. It was time to go home.

"I guess[1] you want the whole[2] day tomorrow," Scrooge said angrily to his clerk. "You want to sit at home all day[3] and still get paid[4]?"

"Well, yes, sir, if it isn't a bother[5]. It is Christmas." Bob was worried about[6] not being able to[7] be with his family.

"Bah, humbug! It is a bother. Every year on December 25th, you don't work, but I have to pay you. It's money for nothing[8]!"

Bob just looked down, holding[9] his hat tightly[10] in his hands.

"All right, I have no choice. But be here early on the 26th."

"Yes, sir. Thank you, sir." Bob left quickly before Scrooge could change his mind[11]. Once[12] he was outside, he forgot all about the work—it was Christmas Eve. He was happy to be going home to his family.

1. **guess** [ges] (v.) 猜測
2. **whole** [houl] (a.) 完整的;全部的
3. **all day** 整天
4. **get paid** 拿到薪水
5. **bother** [ˋbɑːðər] (n.) 困擾
6. **be worried about** 擔心
7. **be able to** 能夠

A Christmas Carol

8. **for nothing** 徒然
9. **hold** [hould] (v.) 抓住；握住
10. **tightly** [`taɪtli] (adv.) 緊緊地
11. **change one's mind**
   改變主意

12. **once** [wʌns] (conj.)
   只要當……之時

A Circle the words best describe the character of Mr. Scrooge.

miserly

lazy

cold

generous

cheerful

mean

foolish

warm

B Match.

1 Bob ·   · ⓐ Scrooge's business partner

2 Fred ·   · ⓑ Scrooge's nephew

3 Marley ·   · ⓒ Scrooge's clerk

C Match.

1 poorhouse ·   · ⓐ a place for children with no families

2 orphanage ·   · ⓑ a place for poor people

3 prison ·   · ⓒ a place for criminals

D Choose the correct answer.

1 Fred came to Scrooge's office _____.

    (a) to make his uncle angry

    (b) to invite him to Christmas dinner

    (c) to give him charcoal for the fire

2 The gentlemen came to Scrooge's office _____.

    (a) to get a donation

    (b) to ask him to pay taxes

    (c) to wish him a merry Christmas

E True or False.

T F **1** Scrooge and Marley worked together for seven years.

T F **2** Christmas was only a time for Scrooge to be generous.

T F **3** Fred felt sorry for Scrooge because Scrooge had no family.

T F **4** Bob didn't have to work on Christmas.

Chapter Two

🎧 7 Marley's Ghost

Bob went home to see his family; Scrooge went back to his empty[1] house. The house was cold and dark. For some people the darkness[2] was scary[3], but Scrooge liked it—it was cheap.

That night when he got home, however[4], the house seemed strange. Maybe it was because it was Marley's house and he had died exactly[5] seven years ago this very[6] day.

Maybe it was just because the heavy fog made it darker than normal[7]. It seemed like there was someone or something else in the house.

---

1. **empty** [ˋempti] (a.) 空的
2. **darkness** [ˋdɑːrknəs] (n.) 黑暗
3. **scary** [ˋskeri] (a.) 嚇人的
4. **however** [hauˋevər] (adv.) 然而
5. **exactly** [ɪgˋzæktli] (adv.) 恰好地；精確地
6. **very** [ˋveri] (a.) 正是；恰好是
7. **normal** [ˋnɔːrməl] (n.) 正常；平常

Scrooge lit[8] a candle and looked around the room.

"Bah, humbug," he said, "no one is here." Still[9], he carefully locked[10] the door and then made a little fire[11] in the fireplace[12].

8. **light** [laɪt] (v.) 點亮
   (light-lit-lit)
9. **still** [stɪl] (adv.) 仍；尚
10. **lock** [lɑ:k] (v.) 上鎖
11. **make a fire** 生火
12. **fireplace** [ˈfaɪərpleɪs] (n.) 壁爐

29

As the fire started to burn[1], Scrooge thought he heard something in the house. He looked around again, but it was just the ticking[2] of the clock.

In the quiet, Scrooge could hear something else. It was far away, but it was coming closer. It sounded like[3] chains[4] being dragged[5] across the floor above.

Scrooge nervously[6] shook[7] his head. "This can't be happening. I must be dreaming," he thought to himself[8].

1. **burn** [bɜːn] (v.) 燃燒
2. **ticking** [tɪkɪŋ] (n.) 滴答響聲
3. **sound like** 聽起來像
4. **chain** [tʃeɪn] (n.) 鎖鍊；鐐銬
5. **drag** [dræg] (v.) 拖；拉
6. **nervously** [ˋnɜːvəsli] (adv.) 緊張地
7. **shake** [ʃeɪk] (v.) 搖動
8. **think to oneself** 獨自想
9. **doorbell** [ˋdɔːrbel] (n.) 門鈴

Just then the doorbell[9] began to ring loudly. Scrooge wasn't dreaming. Slowly, something came into the room. It wore Marley's old clothes, while its whole body was wrapped[10] in a chain. Many familiar[11] things were attached[12] to the chain—the account books[13], heavy cashboxes[14], keys and locks. But the most familiar thing of all was the face.

The face! He recognized[15] it right away as Marley's.

10. **wrap** [ræp] (v.) 包裹；包起
11. **familiar** [fə`mɪliər] (a.) 熟悉的
12. **attach** [ə`tætʃ] (v.) 附著；繫
13. **account book** 帳本
14. **cashbox** [kæʃbɑ:ks] (n.) 錢箱
15. **recognize** [`rekəgnaɪz] (v.) 認出

One Point Lesson

◊ "This **can't** be happening. I **must** be dreaming," he thought to himself.
「這不可能發生，我一定是在作夢。」他獨自想著。

---

can't : 不可能
must : 一定是（表肯定推測）

e.g. He **can't** be a thief. 他不可能是小偷。
She **must** be sick. 她一定是生病了。

31

9

"Who are you?" asked Scrooge. "Ask not who I am, ask who I was."

"Who were you?" Scrooge cried out. "What do you want from me?"

"You know who I am. I can see it in your eyes."

"It can't be you. That's impossible," Scrooge said. "No! Scrooge, you know it is I, Jacob Marley, your old business partner!" The ghost[1] shouted in anger[2].

1. **ghost** [goʊst] (n.) 鬼魂
2. **in anger** 發怒的
3. **sudden** [`sʌdən] (a.) 突然的
4. **loud** [laʊd] (a.) 大聲的；響亮的
5. **noise** [nɔɪz] (n.) 聲音；噪音
6. **scare** [sker] (v.) 驚嚇
7. **frighten** [`fraɪtən] (v.) 使害怕；使畏懼
8. **tremble** [`trembəl] (v.) 震顫；發抖
9. **grow** [groʊ] (v.) 增加；漸漸變得
10. **fear** [fɪr] (n.) 恐懼；害怕

The sudden[3] loud[4] noise[5] scared[6] Scrooge. He didn't want to believe it, but looking into those cold eyes frightened[7] him. He didn't know how or why, but he knew it was Marley. Scrooge began to be very afraid.

"Yes, I know it is you, Jacob. Why are you here? What do you want?" Scrooge's voice trembled[8] as he spoke. His heart grew[9] cold with fear[10].

33

"If a man stays away from[1] other people while he is alive[2], that man becomes like me," the ghost answered shaking its chain sadly.

"Though I am dead, I must walk through the world of the living. I can see people laugh, but I cannot laugh with them. Happiness, sadness[3], joy[4]—I can see them all, but none of them are for me."

1. **stay away from** 遠離
2. **alive** [əˋlaɪv] (a.) 活著的
3. **sadness** [ˋsædnəs] (n.) 悲傷；悲哀
4. **joy** [dʒɔɪ] (n.) 喜悅
5. **sorrow** [ˋsɑːroʊ] (n.) 悲痛；遺憾
6. **pain** [peɪn] (n.) 痛苦

"But why are you here, before me?" Scrooge's voice shook as he spoke. "And why are you wearing that chain?"

"This chain, this heavy chain of sorrow[5] and pain[6]? You have one just like it, Ebenezer Scrooge. Only yours is far[7] longer and far heavier," the ghost said.

"This is the chain I made during my lifetime. Every time I refused[8] to help those in need[9], the chain became a little longer. When I died, our chains were about the same, Scrooge, but now, after seven years, yours is so much longer than mine."

"But what can I do, Jacob? Please, tell me what I can do," Scrooge was now begging[10] for help.

---

7. **far** [fɑːr] (adv.)
   極;至很高程度
8. **refuse** [rɪˋfjuːz] (v.) 拒絕

9. **in need** 需要;缺乏
10. **beg** [beg] (v.) 乞求
    (beg-begged-begged)

"I cannot stay, Scrooge. I must be going, with no rest[1], no peace," the ghost said as he began to float away[2]. "But wait, please! Tell me what I must do."

"Before I go, I will tell you one thing. That is why I came tonight, Scrooge," the ghost said.

"You will be visited[3] by three ghosts. The first will come tonight at one o'clock. The second will visit tomorrow night at the same time. And the third will come the night after that."

The ghost began floating out the window.

1. **rest** [rest] (n.) 休息；停止
2. **float away** 飄走
3. **visit** [ˋvɪzɪt] (v.) 拜訪
4. **toward** [tɔːrd] (prep.) 朝；向
5. **with that** 接著就
6. **disappear** [dɪsəˋpɪr] (v.) 消失

"But wait, will I see you again? Can't you tell me more?" Scrooge cried as he ran toward[4] the window.

"No, Scrooge, you won't see me again. Remember what I have told you, about the three other ghosts and about not helping others . . ., or you will soon see your own heavy chain." With that[5] the ghost disappeared[6] into the dark night.

One Point Lesson

◆ Remember what I **have told** you. 記住我告訴你的事。

---

have + 過去分詞：現在完成式，用來表示持續到現在或現在才停止的活動。

I **have already read** three books. 我已經讀了三本書。
I've **never seen** a white tiger. 我從來沒有看過白老虎。

As Scrooge came to the window to see where Marley had gone, he suddenly heard some crying down below[1]. Again Scrooge's heart froze[2].

The voices came not from people, but from ghosts. All of them were crying from pain and loneliness[3]. They were following people and trying to help them, but nothing they did could help the living[4].

He quickly closed the window.

"Bah," he thought. "This couldn't have[5] happened. I will go to sleep, and tomorrow everything will be fine."

He checked twice to see if the door was locked and then fell into[6] a troubled[7] sleep.

1. **below** [bɪˋlou] (adv.)
   在下面；在樓下
2. **freeze** [friːz] (v.) 呆住；戰慄
   (freeze-froze-frozen)
3. **loneliness** [ˋlounlɪnəs] (n.)
   孤獨；寂寞
4. **the living** 活著的人
5. **couldn't have** 不可能。
   表對過去事件的猜測或懷疑
6. **fall into a sleep** 沉入夢鄉
7. **troubled** [ˋtrʌbəld] (a.) 不安的

A Rearrange the sentences in chronological order.

1. Scrooge heard many voices crying down below.
2. Scrooge recognized the face as Marley's.
3. Scrooge went to his empty house.
4. Scrooge felt something strange.
5. Marley's ghost began floating away.

_____ ⇨ _____ ⇨ _____ ⇨ _____ ⇨ _____

B Fill in the blanks with the given words.

light   cost   wear   freeze   shake

1. Warmth and light _____ money because they require candles and charcoal.
2. Scrooge _____ a candle and looked around the room.
3. Scrooge angrily _____ his head.
4. The ghost _____ Marley's old clothes.
5. Scrooge's heart _____ when he heard the cries from the ghosts.

C Complete the sentences with "cannot" or "must" according to the given situation.

1 Sally studied very hard.

⇨ She _____ fail in the examination.

2 Tim is making three sandwiches for himself.

⇨ He _____ be hungry.

3 Karen is honest. She never tells a lie.

⇨ She _____ be a liar.

D Choose the correct answer.

1 What does the chain attached to Marley's body mean?

(a) Happiness and joy.

(b) Sorrow and pain.

(c) Peace and curse.

2 What did Marley's ghost warn Scrooge about?

(a) If he ignored those in need, he would lose all his money.

(b) If he didn't love anyone soon, he couldn't marry during his life.

(c) If he didn't help others, his chain would become longer.

American Christmas Party

Americans usually spend the Christmas holidays with their family. Many American families live apart from each other. This is because when the children grow up, they may move to another city or state to go to school or to find a job.

During the Christmas holidays, it is very difficult to get travel reservations because so many people are trying to go to their parent's house.

Mom prepares many kinds of food for the whole family, from salad at the beginning, to ham or turkey for the main course, and usually apple or pumpkin pie for dessert!

Of course, all this takes place after the family has exchanged gifts. Some families open their gifts on Christmas Eve, while other families wait until Christmas morning.

Although many people associate Christmas with Santa Claus and presents, the true meaning of Christmas is to celebrate the baby Jesus' birth, and our love for each other.

· Chapter Three ·

🎧13 The First Spirit[1]

Scrooge opened his eyes. It was still dark.

"Had it all been a dream?" he wondered[2]. "How could Marley have visited me?"

Just then he remembered that the first ghost was to come at one in the morning. Soon he heard the clock strike[3] one.

"Nothing! No one is here," he thought. "It all really was just a bad dream."

Then, just when he thought it was safe, a sudden light filled the room. At the foot of[4] his bed he could see a white figure[5]. Its face seemed young, but its clothes were all white.

---

1. **spirit** [`spɪrɪt] (n.) 幽靈
2. **wonder** [`wʌndər] (v.)
   納悶；懷疑
3. **strike** [straɪk] 時鐘報時
   (strike-struck-struck)
4. **at the foot of** 在……尾端
5. **figure** [`fɪgjər] (n.) 人影
6. **past** [pæst] (n.) 昔日；過去
7. **lead** [liːd] (v.) 帶路；領導
8. **pull out** 往外拉

"You . . . are you the first spirit?" Scrooge asked.

"Yes, I am," the ghost answered quietly. "I am the Ghost of Christmas Past[6]."

"Whose past?"

"Your past." The ghost led[7] him to the window and then started to pull him out[8].

Suddenly they were standing in the country[1]. It was a beautiful winter day.

"This . . . this is where I was born," Scrooge cried. And he remembered the happiness and joy when he was a child.

"Are you sad?" asked the ghost.

"No, no, I am . . . happy," Scrooge said.

"Then why do you cry?"

"I am not crying," Scrooge answered, but he could feel tears[2] on his cheek[3].

1. **country** [ˋkʌntri] (n.) 鄉村
2. **tear** [tɪr] (n.) 眼淚；淚珠
3. **cheek** [tʃi:k] (n.) 臉頰
4. **in the distance** 在遠處
5. **real** [ri:əl] (a.) 真實的
6. **just as** 恰與……一樣
7. **townspeople** [ˋtaʊnzpi:pəl] (n.) 市民；鎮民

Slowly Scrooge and the ghost walked toward a little village. As they came closer, they could hear the happy shouts of children playing in the distance[4]. The boys and girls were coming from a small school. They shouted and laughed happily because it was a holiday.

"They are not real[5]," said the ghost. "They are only spirits from Christmas past. They cannot see us."

But Scrooge knew the spirits, just as[6] he knew the streets, the houses, and the townspeople[7].

◦ This is **where** I was born.
這裡就是我出生的地方。

where: 當作關係代名詞，指稱前面的地點或狀況。

e.g. This is **where** we live. 這裡是我們居住的地方。
That is **where** he was hiding. 那邊就是他躲藏的地點。

"Come," said the ghost. "There is still one child left at the school."

"I know," said Scrooge sadly. "I know." And the ghost could see tears in Scrooge's eyes.

The school was cold and dark now. One little boy sat reading at a desk. Scrooge sat down at a desk next to[1] him and began to cry.

"It's, it's me," Scrooge said. "Once, when I was a boy, I was left alone[2] here on Christmas. My father and mother weren't at home. Now, suddenly, I wish I had . . ." Scrooge's voice grew quiet.

"What? What do you wish?" the ghost asked politely[3].

1. **next to** 緊鄰著
2. **be left alone** 被獨自留下
3. **politely** [pə`laɪtli] (adv.) 禮貌地
4. **heavy** [`hɛvi] (a.) 沈重的
5. **get angry** 發怒
6. **tell A to** 叫 A 去做……
7. **I wish I had** + 過去分詞 我希望當初有
8. **It's time to . . .** 該……的時間

A Christmas Carol

"Nothing, it's too late now," Scrooge said with heavy[4] sadness. "It's just that last night a young boy came to my office window and sang me a Christmas carol. But I gave him nothing. I just got angry[5] and told him to[6] leave. Now, I wish I had[7] given him something . . ."

The ghost smiled. "It's time to[8] see another Christmas."

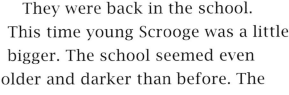

16

They were back in the school. This time young Scrooge was a little bigger. The school seemed even older and darker than before. The one thing that had remained[1] the same was Scrooge sitting all alone at a desk.

Just then the door opened and a young girl ran in. "Ebenezer, it's me, your sister Fran!" said the girl as she ran up to Scrooge and hugged[2] him. "Father is kinder now. He has changed his mind. He wants you to come home."

"I can go home?" young Scrooge asked with a surprised voice. "Father wants me home?"

1. **remain** [rɪˋmeɪn] (v.)
   仍是；保持
2. **hug** [hʌg] (v.) 擁抱
3. **scene** [siːn] (n.) 景象；場面

4. **the same . . . as . . .**
   和⋯⋯一樣⋯⋯
5. **spirit** [spɪrɪt] (n.) 精神；特質

As the old Scrooge watched the scene[3], another tear ran down his cheek. It really had been a merry Christmas that year.

"My sister Fran was a good woman," Scrooge said, "always happy and kind to everyone."

"She had a child, didn't she?" the ghost asked, "before she died?"

"Yes, ghost, she did, my nephew Fred. He has the same[4] happy, kindly spirit[5] as my sister." He remembered[6] seeing Fred earlier that day and refusing[7] his invitation[8] to dinner. It made[9] him feel even worse[10].

6. **remember + V-ing**
   記得;回憶起
7. **refuse** [rɪ`fjuːz] (v.) 拒絕
8. **invitation** [ɪnvɪ`teɪʃən] (n.) 邀請

9. **make** [meɪk] (v.) 使得
10. **worse** [wɜːrs] (a.)
    更壞的;更糟的

51

Now the ghost led Scrooge to a busy, crowded[1] city. They walked up to an office.

"Do you remember this place?" the ghost asked.

"Of course," Scrooge cried happily. "It's old Mr. Fezziwig's office. It's the first place I worked. Mr. Fezziwig was such[2] a happy, kind boss[3]."

1. **crowded** [ˋkraʊdɪd] (a.)
   擁擠的；擠滿人群的

2. **such** [sʌtʃ] (a.)
   這樣的；如此的

3. **boss** [bɔːs] (n.) 老闆

The ghost and Scrooge walked into the office. A fat, happy-looking man sat working at his desk in his office. Suddenly he called out[4] to his two employees[5].

"Dick, Ebenezer!" he shouted. "It's Christmas Eve. It's time to stop working and start celebrating[6]!"

Dick and Scrooge excitedly[7] put away[8] their account books and papers[9] and built a big fire[10].

"I remember Dick," old Scrooge said. "He was my best friend."

Just then Mrs. Fezziwig and the three Fezziwig daughters came into the office. They were followed[11] by even more young people. People talked to their friends, danced[12] to the music, and ate some wonderful food.

4. **call out** 大叫
5. **employee** [ɪmˋplɔɪi] (n.)
   雇員；員工
6. **celebrate** [ˋsɛlɪbreɪt] (v.) 慶祝
7. **excitedly** [ɪkˋsaɪtɪdli] (adv.)
   令人興奮地
8. **put away** 收起；放下
9. **papers** [ˋpeɪpərz] (n.) 文件
10. **build a fire** 生火
11. **follow** [ˋfɑːloʊ] (v.)
    跟隨；隨後
12. **dance** [dæns] (v.) 跳舞

Scrooge enjoyed watching the party. "I used to[1] be different," he thought to himself.

"Everyone loved Mr. Fezziwig," the ghost said. "Why? That party was nothing special[2]. Perhaps they were fools to be so happy over such a small thing . . ."

"No, ghost! You are wrong!" Scrooge said. "Mr. Fezziwig was our boss, so he could make us happy or unhappy. He could make our work easy or hard. And this party was very special to us. It made us happy, and that was even better than money!" Scrooge was surprised when he said that.

1. **used to + V** 過去習慣做……
2. **special** [`speʃəl] (a.) 特別的
3. **bother** [`bɑːðər] (v.)
   使困惑；使不安

"What are you thinking?" the ghost asked. He could see something was bothering[3] Scrooge.

"I was thinking of my clerk, Bob Cratchit," Scrooge said.

"Come, there isn't much time," the ghost said. "We have other Christmases to see."

◆ I **used to** be different. 我過去很不一樣。

used to + 動詞原形：用來表示過去的習慣，同時該習慣目前已經不存在。

e.g. He **used to** be diligent. 過去他很勤奮。
There **used to** be an apple tree here.
這裡以前有一棵蘋果樹。

The scene[1] changed again. Scrooge saw a man of forty[2]. It was himself. He could see the changes time had made. The love of money was now very clear[3].

"Kind ghost, please, I don't want to see anymore!" Scrooge cried because he remembered the scene.

1. **scene** [si:n] (n.) 景象
2. **a man of forty** 40 歲的男人
3. **clear** [klɪr] (a.) 顯而易見的
4. **once** [wʌns] (adv.) 從前
5. **fiancee** [fi:ɑːnˋseɪ] (n.) 未婚妻
6. **be gone** 消失；過去
7. **since** [sɪns] (conj.) 既然；由於
8. **good luck** 祝福好運
9. **in pain** 痛苦地
10. **hurry** [ˋhɝːri] (v.) 催促

Scrooge was sitting with a young woman. The woman had once[4] been his fiancee[5]. She was crying.

"No, it is too late," she said. "You have another love now."

"What? What other love?" this Scrooge asked.

"Money," the woman answered. "You love only money now, not me. Once, when we first met, I believe you loved me. But that is gone[6]. Since[7] I have no money, you have no love for me. Goodbye and good luck[8] with your money."

"Please ghost, no more! I want to go home," Scrooge cried in pain[9] and sadness.

"No, Scrooge," the ghost said. "There is one more scene. Hurry[10], for there is little time."

One Point Lesson

Since I have no money, you have no love for me.
因為我沒有錢，所以你也就不再愛我了。

since: 自從。表原因的連接詞

e.g. We have known each other since we were children.
我們在孩童時期就認識彼此了。
Since I don't love him, I can't marry him.
因為我根本不愛他，所以不能嫁給他。

Years had passed since the last[1] scene. There was a beautiful little girl sitting with her mother next to a big fire in a room. The mother was the woman from Scrooge's past. She saw children playing happily.

Just then the father came into the room. His arms were full of[2] Christmas presents[3]. He gave one to each of his children. They laughed and shouted as they opened the presents.

1. **last** [læst] (a.) 上一個
2. **be full of** 充滿
3. **present** [ˋprɛzənt] (n.) 禮物
4. **thank A for B** 為 B 感謝 A

They thanked their mother and father for[4] the presents, and then they went to bed. Now the room was quiet. There was only the man and his wife.

Then the husband spoke to her, "I saw your old friend today, Ebenezer Scrooge. I walked past[5] his office. People say Marley is dying. Poor Scrooge, once[6] Marley is gone, he will have no friends left in the world."

"Ghost! No more, please!" Scrooge cried. "I don't want to see anymore."

"This was your life," the ghost said. "These were the Christmases of your past. How have you lived your life, Ebenezer Scrooge?" the ghost asked. "These things happened and cannot be changed. Only the future can be changed."

Then the ghost disappeared. Scrooge was back in his bed. His heart ached[7].

5. **past** [pæst] (prep.) 經過
6. **once** [wʌns] (conj.) 一旦
7. **ache** [eɪk] (v.) 疼痛

A True or False.

T F ❶ The first spirit who visited Scrooge was the Ghost of Christmas Past.

T F ❷ The first place where Scrooge and the ghost went was Scrooge's hometown.

T F ❸ When he was a boy, Scrooge was at home with his family on Christmas.

T F ❹ Scrooge didn't enjoy Christmas when he worked in Mr. Fezziwig's office.

T F ❺ Scrooge's fiancee left him because she met a richer man.

B Fill in the blanks with the given words.

with	of	for	on

❶ I never make money _____ Christmas day because no one ever works.

❷ Goodbye and good luck _____ your money.

❸ They thanked their parents _____ the presents.

❹ His arms were full _____ Christmas presents.

C Match.

1. The country where he was born •

2. The child left at the school •

3. Mr. Fezziwig's party •

• a He remembered every-one and everything.

• b He enjoyed watching it.

• c He remembered his sister, Fran.

D Choose the correct answer.

1. "Rise and take my hand," the ghost said. Scrooge did as he _____.

   (a) told   (b) was told

2. "I used _____ different," he thought to himself.

   (a) to be   (b) be

3. _____ I have no money, you have no love for me.

   (a) Since   (b) Though

Chapter Four

The Ghost of Christmas Present[1]

Scrooge woke up and sat up[2] in bed. He heard the church clock. It was one in the morning again— time for the second ghost.

From the next room, he saw a strong light under the door. Slowly Scrooge walked to the door and opened it.

On the couch[3] in the center of the room sat the ghost. He was large and heavy, with a bright cheerful[4] smile on his face. He looked different from[5] ghosts Scrooge knew.

1. **present** [ˋprezənt] (n.) 現在
2. **sit up** 坐直
3. **couch** [kautʃ] (n.) 沙發
4. **cheerful** [ˋtʃɪrfəl] (a.) 愉快的；情緒佳的
5. **different from** 與……不同
6. **grab** [græb] (v.) 抓住

"I am the Ghost of Christmas Present," said the ghost. "Tonight you will come with me and learn from what I show you,"

"Yes," answered Scrooge. "I want to learn. The ghost last night showed me many things. Now I want to see more."

The ghost grabbed[6] Scrooge's hand, and they were gone.

Soon they were at Bob Cratchit, his clerk's house. Mrs. Cratchit was setting the table[1] for Christmas dinner with her daughters. They were excited and happy as the delicious smell of Christmas dinner spread[2] throughout[3] their small, clean home.

Just then Bob Cratchit was coming back from church with the youngest son, Tiny[4] Tim. Tiny Tim was a very special young boy. He was small for his age[5], and he couldn't walk without the use of crutches[6].

1. **set the table** 擺置餐桌
   (set-set-set)
2. **spread** [spred] (v.)
   散布；傳播
   (spread-spread-spread)
3. **throughout** [θruˋaʊt] (prep.)
   遍及；遍布
4. **tiny** [ˋtaɪnɪ] (a.)
   極小的；微小的

"Merry Christmas, everyone!"
Bob said. "What is that
delicious smell?"

"That's the Christmas
goose[7], Father!" The younger
children shouted. No one
said the goose seemed very
small for such a large family.

The family all sat down for their dinner as
Scrooge and the ghost watched. Though it was a
very simple Christmas meal[8], the family was
loving[9] and happy.

After dinner, they all gathered[10] around the
fire. Tiny Tim sat very close to[11] the fire. He was
very sick.

5. **for one's age**
   以個人的年紀來看
6. **crutch** [krʌtʃ] (n.) 柺杖
7. **goose** [guːs] (n.) 鵝
8. **meal** [miːl] (n.) 一餐

9. **loving** [ˋlʌvɪŋ] (a.) 慈愛的
10. **gather** [ˋgæðər] (v.) 聚集
11. **close to** 接近於

23

"Please ghost, tell me," asked Scrooge.
"Will Tiny Tim live?"

"The future can be changed," said the ghost,
"but right now I see only an empty[1] chair where
Tiny Tim is sitting." Scrooge looked very sad
when he heard these words[2].

"But why do you care[3]?"
the ghost asked. "Didn't you
say there were too many
people in the world? Isn't
Tiny Tim dying a good thing
for you?"

Scrooge remembered what he had told the two
gentlemen in his office. He felt ashamed[4].

1. **empty** [ˋempti] (a.) 空的
2. **word** [wɜːd] (n.) 話語；消息
3. **care** [ker] (v.) 關心；在乎
4. **ashamed** [əˋʃeɪmd] (a.)
   羞愧的

5. **drink to** 為……乾杯
6. **miser** [ˋmaɪzər] (n.)
   吝嗇鬼；守財奴

Just then he heard Bob saying his name. "Let's drink to[5] Mr. Scrooge," Bob said.

"To Scrooge?!" his wife answered angrily. "Why should we drink to that old miser[6]?"

"Because it is Christmas," Bob answered.

"Well, you are right," answered his wife. "I'll drink to him. But nothing we say or do could make that mean old man feel happy or merry."

One Point Lesson

Scrooge remembered **what he had told** the two gentlemen in his office.
施顧己想起自己在辦公室裡對那兩位紳士所說的話。

what 在此處當**關係代名詞**，也是被指涉的對象，此時 what 相當於 **the thing(s) that**。

e.g She always does **what she says**.
她總是說到做到。

24

The ghost led him down the street. Everywhere[1] they went, they could hear the happy shouts of people wishing each other a merry Christmas. Soon they came to another home he knew.

He and the ghost entered the bright[2], warm room where the family was sitting. Everyone in the room was laughing at a story his nephew was telling.

"So when I told my Uncle Scrooge 'Merry Christmas,' he just said, 'bah, humbug.'" Fred was telling about his visit to Scrooge's office.

"I think he actually[3] believes it, too," the nephew said. "Can you imagine[4]? Christmas a humbug."

"I never liked that mean[5] old man," Fred's wife said. "He's rich, but he helps no one. He even lives like[6] he's poor."

1. **everywhere** [ˈɛvrɪwɛr] (adv.) 每一處；到處
2. **bright** [braɪt] (a.) 明亮的；光亮的
3. **actually** [ˈæktʃʊəli] (adv.) 真地
4. **imagine** [ɪˈmædʒɪn] (v.) 想像
5. **mean** [miːn] (a.) 難伺候的；刻薄的
6. **like** [laɪk] (conj.) 像；如同

🎧 25

Next they started a game. The game was called[1] 'Twenty Questions[2].' Each person had to think of something, while the others asked them questions. They tried to guess[3] what the person was thinking.

When it was Fred's turn[4], everyone asked him questions.

"Is it an animal?" one guest asked.

"Yes," the nephew answered.

"Does it live in the city?" another asked.

"Yes," the nephew answered again.

The other guests asked questions and learned[5] the animal wasn't a dog or a cat, and that people didn't eat the animal. The animal could talk. Finally it was Fred's wife's turn to ask a question.

1. **be called** 被稱為
2. **Twenty Questions 20個問題**
   一種兩人以上的遊戲，分為問者與答者，首先答者想一個人，但不說出來。問者開始問問題，為了猜出答者所想的人，問者要反覆問各式各樣的問題。如果問了20 個問題仍然沒有猜出，那麼他就輸了。
3. **guess** [gɛs] (v.) 猜測；猜出
4. **turn** [tɜːrn] (n.) 輪流；順序
5. **learn** [lɜːrn] (v.) 得知；獲悉
6. **must be** 一定是
7. **feel bad about** 感到抱歉
8. **vanish** [ˋvænɪʃ] (v.) 消失；突然不見

"Does anyone like it?" she asked.

"No," the nephew answered sadly.

"I know what it is," the wife answered.

"If it is an animal nobody likes, it must be[6] your Uncle Scrooge!" And she was right.

"But I still hope the old man has a merry Christmas and a happy New Year," Fred said, feeling a little bad about[7] his game.

Scrooge wanted to say 'Merry Christmas,' but the scene vanished[8].

As the ghost took him away[1], Scrooge looked at the ghost. The ghost wasn't young anymore. It now looked old.

"Is your life[2] short?" Scrooge asked the ghost.

"Yes, very short," the ghost answered. "It ends Christmas night at midnight. I haven't got[3] much time, but I want to show you one more thing before I go."

The ghost pointed to[4] two children. They were very thin and shook from the cold weather. When Scrooge looked at their eyes, he could see they were sad and very hungry. Their hunger[5] made them look like little monsters[6].

1. **take A away** 將 A 帶走
2. **life** [laɪf] (n.) 生命
3. **have got** 有 (= have)
4. **point to** 指向
5. **hunger** [`hʌŋgər] (n.) 飢餓
6. **monster** [`mɑːntstər] (n.) 怪物；行為、性格異常之人

"They have no mother and no father," the ghost said. "They have no food and no family. They have no money for school. They know nothing and have nothing, and they will always know nothing and have nothing."

"But won't someone help them?" Scrooge cried. "Are there no orphanages?" the ghost asked.

"Ah, why should anyone help? There are too many people in the world already . . ."

Just then the church clock struck twelve. Scrooge looked for the ghost, but it was gone.

A Match.

1 I never liked that mean old man. •   • a The Ghost

2 Will Tiny Tim live? •   • b Bob

3 Let's drink to Mr. Scrooge. •   • c Scrooge

4 The future can be changed •   • d Fred's wife

5 I feel sorry for him. •   • e Fred

B True or False.

T F 1 The Ghost of Christmas Present lives a long time.

T F 2 Bob's family was unhappy because the meal was very simple.

T F 3 Scrooge watched the party at Bob Cratchit's house with sadness.

T F 4 Fred was happy when his wife gave the right answer.

T F 5 The two children in the street had no one to care about them.

C Fill in the blanks with the given words.

crutch　goose　monsters　miser　couch

❶ On the _____ in the center of the room sat the ghost.

❷ Tiny Tim couldn't walk without help from a _____.

❸ Mrs. Cratchit was cooking the Christmas _____.

❹ Why should we drink to that old _____ ?

❺ Their hunger made them look like little _____.

D Fill in the blanks with proper words.

❶ Leave now. _____ you'll miss the train.

❷ It's _____ for us to ask questions.

London in Dickens' Time

London in Scrooge's time was in the middle of growing pains brought on by the Industrial Revolution. Factories became commonplace, and so did the idea of working in an office all day long for low wages. Families were very large, with ten or more children in most!

For the poor, these were very terrible times. Crowded conditions made pollution terrible. The streets smelled bad from all the garbage. There was no clean water to drink or cook with. These conditions helped diseases spread quickly, and many people died.

Because most families were large and poor, it was common for children to work 16-hour days in factories. Many people had to borrow money and it was very difficult to pay the money back. So many people went to prison because they could not pay their debts.

Chapter Five

The Ghost of Christmas Future

S crooge saw the next ghost coming toward him. Unlike[1] the others, Scrooge couldn't see this one's face or body. He could only see that it was very tall. It wore long black clothes with a black hood[2].

"Are you the Ghost of Christmas Future?" Scrooge asked, his voice shaking[3] slightly[4].

The ghost didn't answer. A long, white hand came out of the clothes and signaled[5] yes.

"Will you show me the future?" Scrooge asked. Again the ghost didn't answer. This time it simply started to walk away[6].

1. **unlike** [ʌnˋlaɪk] (prep.)
   不像；和……不同
2. **hood** [hʊd] (n.)
   （連在斗蓬上的）兜帽
3. **shake** [θeɪk] (v.) 震動；顫抖

4. **slightly** [ˋslaɪtli] (adv.)
   些微地；稍微地
5. **signal** [ˋsɪgnəl] (v.)
   以信號傳達
6. **walk away** 走開

Soon they were in the center of the city. The first place they went was popular among businessmen[7]. They walked around in expensive suits[8] with their hands in their pockets. Scrooge could hear some of them talking.

"All I know," said the fattest businessman, "is that he died on Christmas Eve."

"What about[9] his money?" another man asked.

"No one knows," another answered. "But the funeral[10] will certainly be very small. No one liked him."

---

7. **businessman** [ˋbɪznəsmən] (n.) 商人；生意人
8. **suit** [suːt] (n.) 西裝
9. **what about** 如何？
10. **funeral** [ˋfjuːnərəl] (n.) 葬禮

One Point Lesson

● They walked around in expensive suits **with their hands in their pockets.**
他們穿著昂貴的西裝，手插在口袋裡四處走動。

with + 受詞 + 動詞：形容狀態或樣子。

e.g. He stood **with his mouth open.**
他張大嘴巴站著。

"Who were they talking about?" Scrooge asked.

The ghost didn't answer. He simply led Scrooge to a poor part of the city. Here the streets were very crowded, narrow and dirty. The people were very different from the well-dressed[1] businessmen Scrooge had just seen.

They went into one of the small, dirty shops. The shop had many old things; old clothes, old keys and chains, old plates and old dishes. Scrooge realized it was a place people came to sell their things when they needed money.

1. **well-dressed** [wel`drest] (a.) 穿得很體面的
2. **owner** [`ounər] (n.) 店家
3. **hold onto** 握緊

The owner[2], Joe, sat smoking behind a dirty desk. An old woman was standing in front of him holding onto[3] a big box.

"Give me some money, Joe. I brought you some good things this time."

Joe opened the box and looked inside. "Bed-curtains[4]?" Joe said with a surprised voice. "You took them from his bed—the bed he died in?"

"Sure, why not[5]? He doesn't need them anymore," the old woman answered. "I've also got the expensive shirt the body wore at his funeral."

4. **bed-curtain** 床帘

5. **Why not?** 何不？

🎧 29

Just then another woman walked into the shop carrying even more things. She had been the old man's housekeeper[1].

"Hurry, Joe, and look in my bag. Tell me how much money you can give me for these things," the housekeeper said greedily[2].

He checked every item very carefully. Finally he took two pieces of paper and wrote down some numbers. He gave one paper to each woman and told them, "This is how much I'll give you. This is all I will give, nothing more."

It wasn't a lot of money, but it was certainly more than their old boss had given the women for their hard work.

"It's funny," Joe said. "The old man worked hard his whole life to get rich, but in the end[3] all of the profit[4] goes to us!" And each woman gave a cold, mean laugh[5].

1. **housekeeper** [ˋhaʊskiːpər] (n.) 女管家
2. **greedily** [ˋgriːdɪli] (adv.) 貪婪地；貪心地
3. **in the end** 最後
4. **profit** [ˋprɑːfɪt] (n.) 獲利
5. **give a laugh** 發出笑聲

One Point Lesson

He checked **every item** very carefully.
他把每一樣物品都仔細地檢查一遍。

every + 單數名詞：指「每個」的意思，強調對群體中每個成員都適用，需使用單數動詞。

e.g. **Every student** in our school likes Mr. Kim.
我們學校裡的每位學生都很喜歡金老師。

Suddenly the scene changed. Scrooge stood before a bed with no blankets[1] or curtains. The bed only had a thin[2] sheet[3]. Scrooge could see the body[4] of a dead man under the sheet. The ghost pointed for Scrooge to look at the man's face.

"No, ghost, I cannot look," Scrooge said. His voice was shaking with fear.

"It is so sad. This old man died all alone with no one to love him or remember him kindly[5]. He didn't care about people, only money. I will never forget this scene. It is so terrible[6]. Can we please go now?"

1. **blanket** [ˋblæŋkɪt] (n.) 毯子
2. **thin** [θɪn] (a.) 薄的
3. **sheet** [ʃiːt] (n.) 床單
4. **body** [ˋbɑːdi] (n.) 遺體
5. **kindly** [ˋkaɪndli] (adv.) 令人愉悅地；讚賞地
6. **terrible** [ˋterəbəl] (a.) 可怕的；駭人的
7. **come up to** 來到
8. **upstairs** [ʌpˋsterz] (adv.) 在樓上地
9. **roll** [roʊl] (v.) 滾動

The scene changed again. Now they were at Bob Cratchit's house. Scrooge saw Bob coming in. He looked older and very tired. This time there was no Tiny Tim with him. The family came up to[7] him, and he started to cry.

"I miss my little boy. I want to see my little boy," he cried.

Bob walked to Tiny Tim's room upstairs[8]. It was empty. He had died earlier that day, on Christmas. Scrooge could feel tears rolling[9] down his cheeks.

🎧 31

    They were back outside on a city street. Scrooge couldn't forget the death[1] of the old man, though. He still didn't know who it was.

    "Please tell me who the dead man was," Scrooge begged[2] the ghost. The ghost just looked at him quietly and continued to walk. The ghost suddenly stopped at a cemetery[3]. It simply led him to a grave[4].

1. **death** [dɛθ] (n.) 死亡
2. **beg** [bɛg] (v.) 乞求；懇請
3. **cemetery** [ˋsɛməteri] (n.) 墓地
4. **grave** [greɪv] (n.) 墓穴；墓地
5. **fall on one's knees** 跪下
6. **promise** [ˋprɑːmɪs] (v.) 承諾；答應

Head trembling, he looked up and read the name—EBENEZER SCROOGE. Scrooge fell on his knees[5].

"No, no! It cannot be!" he cried. "I promise[6] I will change. Tell me there's still hope. That's why you're showing me, isn't it?"

The ghost said nothing.

"I will celebrate Christmas! I will help people! Please ghost, tell me it is possible to change my future."

But the ghost was gone. Scrooge was back lying under his blankets in his bed.

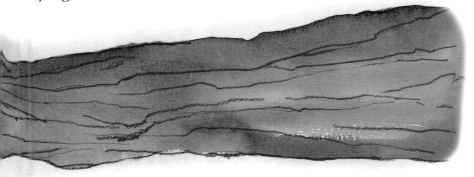

A True or False.

T F ❶ Scrooge couldn't see the face of the ghost of Christmas Future.

T F ❷ The businessmen knew where Scrooge's money was.

T F ❸ People came to Joe's shop to sell things when they needed money.

T F ❹ The name on the grave was "Scrooge and Marley".

B Choose the correct answer.

❶ Scrooge wanted to leave Joe's shop because _____.

(a) there wasn't a lot of money left in the shop

(b) Joe sold his things to the two women

(c) he thought he would die like the old man

❷ At the end of the chapter, Scrooge promised _____.

(a) to become the ghost's friend

(b) to be kind to everyone

(c) to sell his house to help poor people

C Fill in the blanks with the given words.

walk	look	miss	hold	signal

1. A long, white hand came out of the clothes and _____ yes.
2. They _____ around in expensive suits.
3. An old woman was standing in front of him _____ onto a big box.
4. Joe _____ through the bag and the box.
5. I _____ my little boy.
   I want to see my little boy.

D Finish the sentences with the given words.

1. She was running _____

   _____.

   (in / her hands / her pockets / with)

2. They were sitting on the bench _____

   _____.

   (closed / with / their eyes)

Chapter Six

🎧 ³² **Merry Christmas!**

"I still have time!" Scrooge shouted. "I have time to change my life! Thank you, ghosts. I will never forget your lessons¹. Thank you, too, Jacob Marley. You were always a good friend to me!"

Scrooge was very happy to be alive and even happier to have time to change his future.

"What can I do first?" he thought to himself. "Who can I help first?"

He opened the window. It was bright and sunny outside. He saw a young boy walking on the sidewalk⁵ below.

"Excuse me, young man, what day is it?" Scrooge asked the boy. The boy looked surprised. "It's Christmas, sir," the boy answered.

---

1. **lesson** [ˋlɛsn] (n.) 教訓

2. **sidewalk** [ˋsaɪdwɔːk] (n.) 人行道

🎧33

"Christmas!" Scrooge was surprised. All of the visits from the ghosts had taken place[1] in one night.

He called back to the boy, "Young man, do you know the butcher's[2] shop down the street?"

"Of course," answered the boy.

"Good," Scrooge said. "There's a big goose in the window. Do you know if they have sold it?"

"That goose? It's as big as me," the boy answered. "I know they haven't sold it."

"Great," said Scrooge. "Please go and tell the butcher I will buy it. If you come back quickly, I'll give you a nice tip[3]."

1. **take place** 發生
2. **butcher** [ˋbutʃər] (n.) 屠夫
3. **tip** [tɪp] (n.) 小費
4. **huge** [hjuːdʒ] (a.) 極大的
5. **cab** [kæb] (n.) 出租馬車
6. **fare** [fɛr] (n.) 車費

A Christmas Carol

"I'll send the big goose to the Cratchit family,"
he thought to himself.

Soon the butcher and the boy were at Scrooge's
door. The butcher carried the huge[4] goose.
Scrooge gave the boy a nice tip and wished him
"Merry Christmas." Then he paid for the goose,
the cab[5] fare[6] to Cratchit's house, and then gave
the butcher a tip.

One Point Lesson

It's **as big as** me. 它和我一樣大。

「as + 形容詞／副詞 + as + 另一人／物」：像……一樣……。

I am **as tall as** my brother.
我和我兄弟一樣高。

Scrooge put on[1] his best clothes and walked outside. He was smiling and happy. Seeing a happy gentleman, people wished[2] him "Good morning" and "Merry Christmas." Scrooge answered their greetings[3] with his own.

Finally he found who he was looking for—the two gentlemen from the day before.

"Excuse me, sir, do you remember me?" Scrooge asked. "You came to my office yesterday asking me to donate some money to help the poor."

1. **put on** 穿上
2. **wish** [wɪʃ] (v.) 祝福
3. **greeting** [ˋgriːtɪŋ] (n.) 問候
4. **apologize** [əˋpɑːlədʒaɪz] (v.) 道歉
5. **whisper** [ˋwɪspər] (v.) 低語
6. **generous** [ˋdʒenərə] (a.) 慷慨的；博施的
7. **stop by** 順道拜訪

"Ah, yes," one of the men said. "Mr. Scrooge is it?"

"Yes, that's right. I'm very sorry for yesterday," Scrooge said. "I just wanted to apologize[4] and," then Scrooge whispered[5] into the man's ear.

"Really?" The man was surprised. "That's very generous[6] of you! We will be able to help many, many people with that much money."

"Well, just stop by[7] my office tomorrow and I'll give you the money," Scrooge said. "And have a merry Christmas." Then he started walking again.

One Point Lesson

◦ That's very **generous of** you! 您實在是非常慷慨！

用 **kind**、**good**、**foolish** 形容人時，其後所接的介系詞不用 for，而是用 **of**。

e.g. It's very **kind of** you. 您真是有同情心！

35

He kept[1] going until he reached his nephew's house later that afternoon. He was very nervous[2] when he knocked[3] on his nephew's door.

What if[4] he was angry because Scrooge had been rude[5] the day before? What if his nephew's wife didn't want him to come?

Finally a little girl opened the door.

"Hello and Merry Christmas," Scrooge said. "May I come in? I am a friend of your father's."

The girl let him in[6] and took him to the dining room[7]. Everyone was sitting around a nice table that had a lot of Christmas food on it.

"Merry Christmas, everyone!" Scrooge said as he walked in.

"Well, hello, Uncle, Merry Christmas to you, too," Fred answered with a surprised look. "Thank you for coming and joining us."

1. **keep + V-ing** 繼續不斷
2. **nervous** [ˈnɜːrvəs] (a.) 緊張的
3. **knock** [nɑːk] (v.) 敲；擊
4. **what if . . . ?** 假使……呢？
5. **rude** [ruːd] (a.) 無禮的
6. **let A in** 讓 A 進來
7. **dining room** 飯廳
8. **having a good time** 玩得高興

Scrooge sat down and enjoyed one of the happiest Christmases of his life. Everyone had a good time[8] talking to the kind, friendly new Scrooge.

When he left, they thanked him many times for coming and wished him, "Happy New Year."

One Point Lesson

◆ **What if** he was angry because Scrooge had been rude the day before?
要是他因為前一天施顧己的無禮而感到生氣該怎麼辦呢?

What if . . . ? : 假使……怎麼辦?
　→「What will (would) happen if . . . ?」的縮寫

e.g **What if** we are late? 如果我們遲到怎麼辦?
　 What if he doesn't come? 要是他不來呢?

36

The next morning Scrooge went to his office early. He was waiting for his clerk, Bob Cratchit. But Bob didn't come early. Finally Bob came in about fifteen minutes late. Normally[1] this would make Scrooge very angry. Bob quickly went to his desk and started working.

Today wasn't a normal day, though. Scrooge wasn't angry. "Did you have a merry Christmas, Bob?" Scrooge asked.

Bob looked up, surprised. He had expected[2] Scrooge to say something mean.

"Yes, sir, I did," Bob answered. "Some kind person sent us a very big goose to eat for Christmas dinner. It was the best meal my family has had for a long, long time."

1. **normally** [`nɔ:rməli] (adv.)
   通常；按慣例
2. **expect** [ɪk`spekt] (v.)
   料想；以為
3. **secret** [`si:krət] (n.) 秘密
4. **as well** 也；而且
5. **take care of** 照顧

Scrooge was happy to hear that. But he didn't tell Bob he had sent the goose. It was his own secret[3].

"That's nice, Bob," Scrooge said. "I have some news for you as well[4]."

This made Bob very nervous. "Starting today, you will receive more money to take care of[5] your family." Scrooge said with a nice smile. Then Scrooge made a big fire, so they could be warm while they worked.

Tiny Tim did not die. Scrooge became a second father to the family. And he never said, "Humbug" again.

A Rearrange the sentences in chronological order.

1. Scrooge sent Bob a big Christmas goose.

2. Scrooge gave Bob a big raise.

3. Scrooge had Christmas dinner with his nephew.

4. Scrooge found two gentlemen to help him donate money.

5. Scrooge thanked the ghosts for their lessons.

_____ ⇨ _____ ⇨ _____ ⇨ _____ ⇨ _____

B Match.

1. Scrooge got up and _____ his best clothes.   •   •   a   taken place

2. All of the visits from the ghosts had _____ in one night.   •   •   b   stop by

3. _____ my office tomorrow and I'll give you the money.   •   •   c   put on

4. He was very nervous when he _____ his nephew's door.   •   •   d   take care of

5. He gave Bob a higher salary to _____ his family.   •   •   e   knocked on

Appendixes

1. Basic Grammar
2. Guide to Listening Comprehension
3. Listening Guide
4. Listening Comprehension

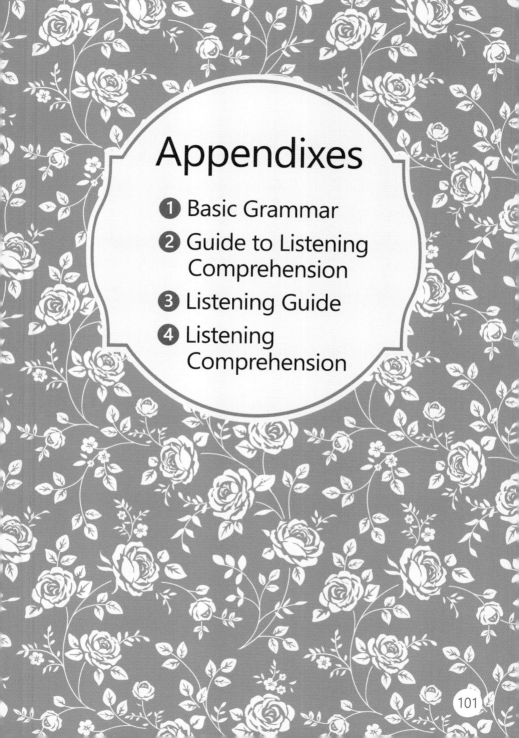

1 Basic Grammar

要增強英文閱讀理解能力，應練習找出英文的主結構。
要擁有良好的英語閱讀能力，首先要理解英文的段落結構。

英文的閱讀理解從「分解文章」開始

英文的文章是以「有意義的詞組」（指帶有意義的語句）所構成的。用（／）符號來區別各個意義語塊，請試著掌握其中的意義。

He knew ／ that she told a lie ／ at the party.

他知道　　　　她說了謊　　　　在舞會上
⇨ 他知道她在舞會上說謊的事。

As she was walking ／ in the garden, ／ she smelled ／

當她行走　　　　　　　在花園　　　她聞到味道

something wet.

某樣東西濕濕的
⇨ 她走在花園時聞到潮溼的味道。

一篇文章，要分成幾個有意義的詞組？

可放入（／）符號來區隔有意義詞組的地方，一般是在（1）「主詞＋動詞」之後；（2）and 和 but 等連接詞之前；（3）that、who 等關係代名詞之前；（4）副詞子句的前後，會用（／）符號來區隔。初學者可能在一篇文章中畫很多（／）符號，但隨著閱讀實力的提升，（／）會減少。時間一久，在不太複雜的文章中即使不畫（／）符號，也能一眼就理解整句的意義。

使用（／）符號來閱讀理解英語篇章
1. 能熟悉英文的句型和構造。
2. 可加速閱讀速度。

該方法對於需要邊聽理解的英文聽力也有很好的效果。
從現在開始，早日丟棄過去理解文章的習慣吧！

以直接閱讀理解的方式，重新閱讀《小氣財神》

從原文中摘錄一小段。以具有意義的詞組將文章做斷句區分，重新閱讀並做理解練習。

A long, long time ago, / Scrooge and Marley had been / good business partners. //
很久很久以前　　　　　施顧己和馬里曾經是　　很好的生意伙伴

Each had tried / to work harder / than the other. //
每人都試著　　　更努力工作　　比另一個人

Each had wanted / to be richer / than the other. //
每人都想　　　　更富有　　比另一個人

Even now, / seven years after Marley had died, / the company was still called / 'Scrooge and Marley.' //
即使現在　　馬里死後七年　　公司依然被稱為　　施顧己與馬里

If you went to their office, / that is what you would see / on the door, / 'Scrooge and Marley.' //
如果你去他們的辦公室　　那就是你會見到的　　　　　在門上
施顧己與馬里

But now / the only owner was Scrooge. //
但是現在　唯一的所有人是施顧己

Scrooge was known / by everyone / to be mean, miserly, and cold. //
施顧己知名的　　　　被所有人　　是刻薄、吝嗇和冷酷

He hated / spending money / and he hated / giving money away
/ even more. // And cold? //
他恨　　　花錢　　　也恨　　　拿錢給人　　更甚　　而冷酷

Scrooge's thin white lips, icy blue nose, and tiny red eyes / showed the cold. //
施顧己蒼白的薄唇、尖刻的青藍色鼻子和小小泛紅的眼睛　　　展現冷酷

His weak, brittle voice could make / you / hear the cold. //
他薄弱冷淡的聲音會讓　　　　　　你　　聽見冷酷

Feeling the cold was the worst / – he kept his office very, very cold, / especially at Christmas. //
感覺寒冷是最糟的　　　　　　　他讓他的辦公室裡非常非常冷
特別是在聖誕節

He hated / to buy charcoal / for the fire, / so his office was always cold and dark. //
他討厭　　買木炭　　　加進火裡　所以他的辦公室裡總是寒冷又黑暗

Though it was only three o'clock in the afternoon, / it was already getting dark / because of the heavy, wet fog. //
雖然現在才下午三點　　天色已經變暗　因為濃濃的濕霧

The only other person / in the office / was Bob Cratchit, Scrooge's clerk. //

唯一的另一個人　　　在辦公室　　　是鮑伯・克來契，施顧己的職員

Bob was sitting / next to a tiny fire. //

鮑伯正坐著　　　小火旁邊

He tried warming his hands / over the candle / he was using for light, / but that couldn't help. //

他想要暖手　在蠟燭上　　　他用來照明的　　　但是卻沒有幫助

Bob went home / to see his family / ; Scrooge went back / to his empty house. //

鮑伯回家　　　看他的家人　　　　施顧己回去　　　他空蕩的房子

The house was cold and dark. //

房裡寒冷與黑暗

For some people / the darkness was scary, / but Scrooge liked it / — it was cheap. //

對一些人而言　　黑暗很可怕　　但施顧己喜歡　　它很便宜

That night / when he got home, / the house seemed strange. //

那一晚　　當他到家　　　　房子看起來很奇怪

Maybe it was / because it was Marley's house / and he had died / exactly seven years ago / this very day. //

可能是　　　　　　　　因為這是馬里的房子　　　而且他死去
　　　正好七年前　　　　　就在今天

Maybe it was / just because the heavy fog made it darker / than normal. //

可能是　　　只因為濃霧讓它變得更暗　　比平常

Guide to Listening Comprehension

When listening to the story, use some of the techniques shown below. If you take time to study some phonetic characteristics of English, listening will be easier.

Get in the flow of English.

English creates a rhythm formed by combinations of strong and weak stress intonations. Each word has its particular stress that combines with other words to form the overall pattern of stress or rhythm in a particular sentence.

When you are speaking and listening to English, it is essential to get in the flow of the rhythm of English. It takes a lot of practice to get used to such a rhythm. So, you need to start by identifying the stressed syllable in a word.

Listen for the strongly stressed words and phrases.

In English, key words and phrases that are essential to the meaning of a sentence are stressed louder. Therefore, pay attention to the words stressed with a higher pitch. When listening to an English recording for the first time, what matters most is to listen for a general understanding of what you hear. Do not try to hear every single word. Most of the unstressed words are articles or auxiliary verbs, which don't play an important role in the general context. At this level, you can ignore them.

Pay attention to liaisons.

In reading English, words are written with a space between them. There isn't such an obvious guide when it comes to listening to English. In oral English, there are many cases when the sounds of words are linked with adjacent words.

For instance, let's think about the phrase "**take off**," which can be used in "take off your clothes." "Take off your clothes" doesn't sound like [teɪk ɔːf] with each of the words completely and clearly separated from the others. Instead, it sounds as if almost all the words in context are slurred together, [ˈteɪkɔːf], for a more natural sound.

Shadow the voice of the native speaker.

Finally, you need to mimic the voice of the native speaker. Once you are sure you know how to pronounce all the words in a sentence, try to repeat them like an echo. Listen to the book again, but this time you should try a fun exercise while listening to the English.

This exercise is called "shadowing." The word "shadow" means a dark shade that is formed on a surface. When used as a verb, the word refers to the action of following someone or something like a shadow. In this exercise, pretend you are a parrot and try to shadow the voice of the native speaker.

Try to mimic the reader's voice by speaking at the same speed, with the same strong and weak stresses on words, and pausing or stopping at the same points.

Experts have already proven this technique to be effective. If you practice this shadowing exercise, your English speaking and listening skills will improve by leaps and bounds. While shadowing the native speaker, don't forget to pay attention to the meaning of each phrase and sentence.

Step 1

Listen to what you want to shadow many times. Start out by just trying to shadow a few words or a sentence.

Step 2

Mimic the CD out loud. You can shadow everything the speaker says as if you are singing a round, or you also can speak simultaneously with the recorded voice of the native speaker.

Step 3

As you practice more, try to shadow more. For instance, shadow a whole sentence or paragraph instead of just a few words.

以下為《小氣財神》各章節的前半部。一開始若能聽清楚發音，之後就沒有聽力的負擔。先聽過摘錄的章節，之後再反覆聆聽括弧內單字的發音，並仔細閱讀各種發音的說明。

以下都是以英語的典型發音為基礎，所做的簡易說明，即使這裡未提到的發音，也可以配合音檔反覆聆聽，如此一來聽力必能更上層樓。

Chapter One page 14 🎧 37

A long, long time ago, Scrooge and Marley had been good business (❶). Each (❷) (   ) (   ) work harder than the other. Each had wanted to be richer than the other.

Even now, seven years after Marley had died, the company (❸) (   ) called 'Scrooge and Marley.'

❶ partners: 重音在第一音節，其中 -t- 和 -n- 連在一起時，[t] 的音會迅速略過，聽起來像沒有發音。

❷ had tried to: had 字尾的 d 音與 tried 一起唸時，[d] 的發音較弱，口語中往往聽不出來；至於 tried to 的 -d 和 t 可視為一個字，連著發音，此時 [d] 音會不明顯。

❸ was still: was 的 s 和 still 連在一起時，兩個 s 只發音一次；而 s 後面接著的 [d]、[t]、[k] 就變成發輕音。

Chapter Two page 28 🎧 38

Bob (❶) (   ) to see his family; Scrooge went back to his empty house. The house was cold and dark. For some people the darkness (❷) (   ), but Scrooge liked it — it was cheap.
That night when he got home, however, the house seemed strange. Maybe it was because it was Marley's house and he had died exactly seven years ago this very day.

❶ went home: went 和 home 兩個字連在一起唸，t 發出的音很微弱，口語中聽起來會像沒有發音。

❷ was scary: was 的 s 和 scary 連在一起時，兩個 s 只發音一次，若有兩個相同或相似的音連在一起時，通常只發一次音，因此這兩個字聽起來會只有一個 [s] 音。

> Scrooge opened his eyes. It was still dark.
> "Had it all been a dream?" he wondered. "How could
> Marley have (❶) me?" (❷) (   ) he remembered
> that the first ghost was to come at one in the
> morning. Soon he heard the clock strike one.

❶ **visited:** visited 的字尾 -ted，因 [t] 與 [d] 不易同時發音，故 –ed 發 [id] 的音，整個字的發音為 [ˋvɪzɪtɪd]。

❷ **Just then:** just 字尾的 [t] 和 then 的 [ð] 音連在一起發音時，[t] 音會不明顯，口語時通常只聽得到 [ð] 的音。

> Scrooge woke up and (❶) (   ) in bed. He heard
> the church clock. It was one in the morning again —
> time for the second ghost. From the next room, he saw
> a strong light under the door. Slowly Scrooge (❷)
> (   ) the door and opened it.

❶ **sat up:** sat 與 up 兩個字於前後文出現時，形成連音，斷字的方式為 sa tup，這是片語的口語習慣用法。

❷ **walked to:** walked 原本的發音為 [wɔɪkt]，但後面接 to 時與其 [t] 連在一起只發一次音，因此需對照前後文來判斷時態。

Scrooge saw the next ghost coming (❶) (   ). Unlike the others, Scrooge couldn't see this one's face or body. He could only see that it was very tall. It (❷) long black clothes with a black hood.

❶ **toward him:** toward 的美式發音為 [tɔɪrd]，toward 後面緊接著 him，[h] 音會迅速略過與前一個字變成連音，通常以 h 開頭的代名詞，依前後文迅速發弱音時，[h] 因會略過聽不清楚。

❷ **wore:** 口語中的發音類似 were，因此在聽的時候需由前後文判斷究竟應使用哪一個單字。

Chapter Six page 90 🎧42

"I still have time!" Scrooge (❶). "I have time to change my life! Thank you, ghosts. I will never forget your lessons. Thank you, too, Jacob Marley. You were always a good (❷)(   ) me!"

❶ **shouted:** 重音在第一音節，-ou- 發 [au] 的音，字尾的發音為 [tɪd]。

❷ **friend to:** to 除了在特別強調的時候以外，在日常會話中都會變化成 ta 的音，本例中 friend 的 [d] 音略過，只聽得到 [t] 的音。

4

Listening Comprehension

🎧 43 **A** Listen to the CD and fill in the blanks.

1 He always wants everything his way, and he never shares. He is so _____.

2 My family ate both a turkey and a _____ for Christmas dinner.

3 Please go to the _____ and buy some pork and beef.

4 Sammy is my brother's son. He is my _____.

🎧 44 **B** True or False.

T F **1** _____

T F **2** _____

🎧 45 **C** Listen to the CD and choose the correct answer.

1 _____?

   (a) He promised to celebrate it every year.
   (b) He forgot it was Christmas.
   (c) Bah, humbug.

2 _____ ?

    (a) Because it was Christmas.

    (b) Because Scrooge was so kind.

    (c) Because his wife wanted to.

3 _____ ?

    (a) He felt sorry for him.

    (b) He respected him.

    (c) He wanted Scrooge's money.

D Listen to the CD and write down the sentences. Then rearrange the sentences in chronological order.

1 _____

2 _____

3 _____

4 _____

5 _____

_____ ⇨ _____ ⇨ _____ ⇨ _____ ⇨ _____ ⇨ _____

　　查爾斯・狄更斯（Charles Dickens, 1812–1870）是位優秀的英國小說家。因出生貧寒，幼年未能接受正規學校教育。12 歲時，他開始在工廠工作。19 世紀早期，英國資本主義興起，替英國大都市帶來榮景。然而，資本主義也有黑暗面。童工猖獗，勞動階級的人們飽受貧窮之苦。

　　脫胎自對社會正義的自身苦痛經驗，狄更斯具有洞見，並開始著作短篇故事教育自身。他相信對自我教育的追求能帶領他脫離貧苦。

　　因對勞動階級的日常生活刻畫鮮明，狄更斯的小說備愛尊崇。他從親身經歷中深知那些悲喜感受，筆下美麗幽默的人物描繪，也檢視了不公與社會矛盾的狀況。

　　他最廣為人知的作品包括《孤星血淚》（又譯《遠大前程》，Great Expectations）和《孤雛淚》（Oliver Twist）。狄更斯雖時常被批評，指他刻意迎合讀者的多愁善感與愛好浮誇的閱讀品味，但他被尊為偉大英國小說家的原因，如同莎士比亞（Shakespeare），在於其為角色注入的豐富人性與幽默感，展現出真實人類的過錯、堅毅與生命力。

　　狄更斯於 1870 年 6 月 9 日逝世，舉世哀悼，並同其他英國傑出小說家被葬於西敏寺內（Westminster Abbey）。

　　《小氣財神》是 1843 年的不朽佳作，描寫一位名叫施顧己的刻薄守財奴。施顧己是個性惡劣吝嗇的老男人，他認為聖誕節不過是場讓人浪擲錢財的可笑陰謀，直到他看見了已逝的生意伙伴雅各‧馬里的鬼魂，並被告知有個三位幽靈會在聖誕夜拜訪他。

　　果然，在聖誕夜，過去、現在和未來的聖誕幽靈分別前來拜訪施顧己。幽靈們向施顧己展示了他過去、現在與未來的生活方式所犯下的過錯。

　　過去的聖誕幽靈顯現他如何從純真的孩童，長大後逐漸墮落成可悲的小氣鬼；現在的聖誕幽靈顯現他貧窮的員工與姪子的快樂生活；未來的聖誕幽靈帶他去他的墓園，顯現他如何孤老而終。施顧己看見自己貪婪逐利的一生走向悲慘的結尾。

　　幸虧三位幽靈，施顧己在聖誕節早晨清醒後完全蛻變一新，扭轉了自己的生命，成為一個慷慨、善良的人。

　　《小氣財神》為兒童改寫，廣受世人閱讀和喜愛，教導讀者尋找生命真正的幸福。這本名著也為聖誕故事開創了新的文類。

p. 12–13

Scrooge 施顧己

我的名字是艾伯納瑟・施顧己，我生平最痛恨花錢和給別人錢，對於聖誕節，我只有一句話可說，那就是：「呸！騙人的玩意兒！」

Marley 馬里

我是雅各・馬里，過去我和施顧己是生意夥伴。但是很不幸地，我在七年前離開人世，現在，我身上綁著鎖鍊，在人間遊蕩。

Bob Crachit 鮑伯・克來契

我是鮑伯・克來契，是施顧己的職員，我有一個很美滿的家庭，過著幸福的生活。我工作非常認真，但可惜沒有賺到多少錢。

Fred 佛瑞德

我名叫佛瑞德，我是施顧己的外甥，我和我舅舅大相逕庭，我很愛笑，喜歡花時間與我親愛的家人相處，我猜這些特質是遺傳自我母親。

Christmas Ghost of Past 過去的聖誕幽靈

我是過去的聖誕幽靈，我讓施顧己看到他昔日曾過的聖誕節，藉由憶起那些美好的時光，希望能讓他看清自己犯下的錯誤。

Christmas Ghost of Present 現在的聖誕幽靈

　　我是現在的聖誕幽靈，我把今年聖誕節的景象展現給他看，希望能夠説服他改變吝嗇貪婪的習性。

Christmas Ghost of Future 未來的聖誕幽靈

　　我是未來的聖誕幽靈，如果施顧己依然是那個無情無義、刻薄的糟老頭，我會把等在他人生未來的景象讓他瞧瞧。

`p. 14–15`

[第一章] 施顧己

　　在很久以前，施顧己和馬里是一對很好的生意夥伴。他們在工作上比賣力，都想比對方賺更多的錢。

　　即使到了馬里去世七年後的今日，這家公司仍稱為「施顧己·馬里聯合公司」。

　　如果你到他們的辦公室，會在門上看見「施顧己·馬里聯合公司」的招牌，但現在公司的老闆只有施顧己一人。

　　人人都知道施顧己是個刻薄、吝嗇、冷酷無情的人。他討厭花錢，更討厭把捐錢給別人。他是怎麼個冷酷法呢？他有蒼白的薄嘴唇，冰冷發青的鼻子，泛著紅絲的小眼睛，在在顯示出他的冷酷。

　　他虛弱無力的冷淡嗓音，聽起來讓人不寒而慄。忍受寒冷是最糟糕的——他的辦公室裡非常地冷，特別是在聖誕節那段時間。他痛恨買木炭生火，寧可讓辦公室常保冰冷陰暗。

`p. 16–17` 現在時間雖然才下午三點，但濕冷的濃霧已經讓天色黯淡下來，辦公室只剩鮑伯·克來契一個人，他是施顧己的職員。鮑伯坐在一小撮火旁邊，把手放在用來照明的蠟燭上方取暖，但一點用也沒有。

「聖誕快樂，舅舅！」突然冒出一陣愉悅嗓音，那是施顧己年輕的外甥，佛瑞德。

「呸！騙人的玩意兒！」施顧己回答。他工作被打斷，便一臉生氣的模樣。

「騙人的玩意兒？！為什麼您會覺得聖誕節是騙人的玩意，舅舅？」佛瑞德和善地問道：「您該不是認真的吧？每個人都喜歡聖誕節啊！」

「我當然是認真的，」施顧己說，「聖誕快樂，到底有什麼好快樂的？你不夠窮嗎？你有什麼值得快樂的？」

「那麼您又為什麼不快樂呢，舅舅？您可是有錢得不得了啊！」佛瑞德掛著微笑回答。

p. 18–19 施顧己這下可被惹毛了，「世界上有那麼多蠢蛋老在祝福別人『聖誕快樂』，自己卻窮得連一毛錢都沒有！」

「舅舅，拜託你！這可是一年中最美好的時光啊！」

「美好？！好在哪裡？就因為大家都不工作，害我聖誕節沒賺過半毛錢！」施顧己並不明白聖誕節的意義。

「但是聖誕節和錢是沒有關連的啊，舅舅。」佛瑞德說，「我愛聖誕節，這是個表現歡樂與寬容的日子。」

小小辦公室裡的鮑伯也深表同意。「你說得對，先生，祝你聖誕快樂。」

「回去做你的事！」施顧己命令道，「不然你就會丟了飯碗，快樂不起來了。」

「別生氣，舅舅，我只是來邀請您吃聖誕大餐的。」佛瑞德知道舅舅討厭聖誕節，但仍為他感到難過，因為他孤家寡人一個。

「別了，我忙得很，你過你的聖誕節，我過我的，現在給我出去。」

p. 20–21 「您不跟我們一起過節嗎，舅舅？我們是一家人，應該彼此陪伴。」

「再見。」這是施顧己唯一的回答。

「好吧，很遺憾聽到您這麼說，但還是祝您聖誕快樂。」

佛瑞德離開之際，對著還待在冰冷辦公室裡的可憐鮑伯說了聲：「聖誕快樂！」

「是啊，也祝你聖誕快樂！」鮑伯熱情地回答，接著他為佛瑞德打開門，看著他走進霧裡。

「兩個傻瓜互祝聖誕快樂。」施顧己說。

就在此時，兩位穿著昂貴服飾、身材肥胖紳士來到辦公室裡。

「抱歉，請問這裡是施顧己和馬里聯合公司的辦公室嗎？」

「沒錯，這裡就是。」施顧己回答。工作又被打斷，他一臉不悅。

「請問您是施顧己先生還是馬里先生？」其中一人問道。

「馬里先生已經去世了，他是在七年前也就是一八三六年的聖誕夜過世的。」

「喔，我感到很遺憾，」那個人說，「不過我們會在這個一年中最神聖的日子來到這裡，是想請問您是否願意捐些錢給窮苦的人，有太多人在挨餓沒有飯吃。」

p. 22–23 「外面難道沒有監獄嗎？」施顧己問，「還是沒有孤兒院？」

「有的，先生，外面還有很多監獄和孤兒院。」

「還有給窮人住的救濟院呢？」施顧己說著投以鄙視的眼神。

「令人難過的是，外面的確還有很多救濟院、孤兒院和監獄，」說話的還是同一個人，「但是很多人沒有辦法去這些地方，他們飢寒交迫，能不能請您捐一些錢幫助這些人呢？」

「不行，我不會把錢送給懶惰不工作的人。」施顧己說。

「但是，先生，有些人可能會死，難道您不願意幫助他們嗎？」

「我有幫助他們，他們已經從我繳的稅裡享受到很多了，況且現在世界上的人那麼多，死一些懶惰的蠢蛋也是好事一件。」

這兩個人看得出來施顧己絕對不會捐給他們任何東西，便對鮑伯投了一個同情的眼神。

「快回去工作，別再被打斷了！」施顧己對著他的職員吼道。

p.24-25 時間逐漸從午後推移至傍晚，到了該下班回家的時間。

「我猜你明天想要休假一整天，」施顧己火大地對職員說：「你想在家裡坐一整天，就能領到薪水是吧？」

「是的，老闆，如果不會太麻煩的話，因為明天是聖誕節。」鮑伯擔心自己沒辦法陪伴家人。

「呸！什麼騙人的玩意兒！這確實很麻煩，每年一到十二月二十五日，你就不工作，我卻還得付你薪水，花了錢卻什麼也得不到！」

鮑伯只得垂下頭，手中緊緊握著帽子。

「好吧！我也沒有選擇，不過你二十六號早點來上班。」

「是的，老闆。謝謝您！」鮑伯趁施顧己還沒改變主意前趕緊離開。他一出了門，就把工作拋到九霄雲外——今天可是聖誕夜，他很高興要回家和家人團聚。

p. 28–29

［第二章］馬里的鬼魂

鮑伯回家陪伴家人，施顧己則回到他空蕩蕩的屋子，屋裡寒冷陰暗。對有些人來說，陰暗的地方很嚇人，但是施顧己卻很喜歡——因為這樣比較省錢。

不過那一晚他回家時，屋子裡頭似乎感覺有些怪異，或許是因為這以前是馬里的房子，而今天剛好又是他第七年的忌日。也搞不好只是因為霧比較濃，所以天色看起來比較暗，才讓屋子裡感覺好像還有其他什麼人或其他什麼東西的。

施顧己點了一根蠟燭環視屋裡。

「呸！什麼東西！」他說，「根本就沒有人在這兒！」不過他還是小心翼翼地把門鎖起來，在火爐裡生了一點火。

p. 30–31 當爐火開始燃燒，施顧己覺得自己又聽到一些怪聲，他又四處瞧了瞧，發現不過是時鐘滴滴答答的聲音。

在一片寂靜中，施顧己還聽到其他聲音從遠方傳來，而且聲音越來越近，像是有鐵鍊拖過樓上地板的聲音。

施顧己緊張地甩甩頭。「不可能，我一定是在做夢。」他自己想著。

就在這時，門鈴大聲地響起，施顧己並不是在作夢。有個人影緩緩走進屋裡，它穿著馬里的舊衣服，全身拴著鐵鍊，鐵鍊上還掛著許多他很熟悉的物品，包括帳本、重重的錢箱，以及鎖頭和鑰匙，但其中他最熟悉的，是那張臉。

那張臉！他立刻認出，那是馬里的臉。

p. 32–33 「你是誰？」施顧己問。

「不要問我是誰，問問我以前是誰。」

「你以前是誰？」施顧己大喊，「你想對我做什麼？」

「你知道我是誰，我可以從你的眼神看出來。」

「不可能是你！這不可能啊！」施顧己說。

「不，施顧己，你明知道就是我，我是雅各・馬里，你以前的生意夥伴！」鬼魂怒吼著。

突然放大的音量把施顧己嚇了一跳，他不想相信這是真的，卻也不敢看著那雙嚇人的眼睛。他不明白這是怎麼發生的，也不知道為什麼會發生，但他知道那就是馬里，施顧己驚恐了起來。

「是，我知道是你，雅各。你為什麼會在這裡？你到底想要什麼？」施顧己說話的聲音在顫抖，他嚇得心頭一陣冷顫。

p. 34–35 「如果有人在活著的時候遠離人群，就會變得像我一樣。」鬼魂悲哀地甩著鐵鍊。

「雖然我已經死了，卻得在人世間遊蕩。我看得見人們歡笑，卻不能和他們一起笑。歡樂、悲傷、喜悅，我全都能看見，卻沒有一樣是我能感受得到的。」

「但是你為什麼會出現在這裡，在我面前？」施顧己說話的聲音顫抖，「又為什麼戴著那副鐵鍊？」

「這副鐵鍊？這副拖著遺憾與痛苦的沈重鐐銬？你也有一副一模一樣的，艾伯納瑟‧施顧己，只不過你的那副更長、更沈重，」鬼魂說道。

「這副枷鎖是我活著時自己打造的，每當我拒絕幫助那些有需要的人，鐵鍊就會加長一點。在我死時，我們倆的鐵鍊是差不多長的，施顧己，不過現在，七年過去了，你的已經比我的長多了。」

「那怎麼辦，雅各？求求你告訴我該怎麼辦。」現在施顧己開始求他幫忙。

p. 36–37 「我不能留下來，施顧己，我得繼續走下去，永不得安息。」鬼魂說著說著，開始越飄越遠了。

「等一下，拜託！告訴我該怎麼辦！」

「在我走之前，要告訴你一件事，那就是我今晚來的原因，施顧己，」鬼魂說。

「即將會有三個幽靈來找你。第一個幽靈今天凌晨一點會來，第二個幽靈明天會在同樣的時間出現，第三個幽靈則是後天會來。」

鬼魂開始飄出窗外。

「等一下，我還會再見到你嗎？你不能再多說一點嗎？」施顧己大喊著走向窗戶。

「不會，施顧己，你不會再見到我，記住我跟你說的那三個幽靈，還有不幫助別人的下場……，否則你很快就會見到自己那副沈重的鐵鍊。」鬼魂就這麼消失在黑暗的夜色中。

p. 39 施顧己來到窗邊看著馬里消失的地方，突然聽到下方傳來陣陣的哭泣聲，他又一陣哆嗦。

那些不是人類的聲音，而是鬼魂的聲音，他們都因為痛苦和孤獨而哭泣著。他們跟在人們的身後，想要提供幫助，只是他們幫不上活人的忙。

施顧己迅速把窗戶關上。

「唉！」他想，「這不可能是真的，我現在就上床睡覺，明天醒來就什麼事都沒有了。」

他檢查了兩次門鎖，接著便不安地睡下了。

p. 42-43 美式聖誕派對

美國人通常會與家人一起度過聖誕假期，許多美國人並沒有和家人同住，這是因為孩子長大之後，可能會搬到其他州、其他城市去讀書或就業。

一到聖誕假期，就很難訂到車票，因為有太多人要回家探望父母。

媽媽會為全家人準備各種美食，從前菜的沙拉、到主菜的火腿和火雞，而甜點通常是蘋果派或南瓜派。

當然啦，大餐是在全家人交換過禮物之後才享用的，有些家庭會在聖誕夜打開禮物，有些家庭則是會等到聖誕節當天一早才拆禮物。

雖然講到聖誕節，很多人都會聯想到聖誕老公公和聖誕禮物，但聖誕節其實是要慶祝耶穌的誕生，以及人類之間的愛。

p. 44-45

[第三章] 第一個聖誕幽靈

施顧己張看雙眼，天色依然昏暗。

「那是夢吧？」他納悶，「馬里怎麼可能會來看我呢？」

這時他突然憶起第一個幽靈將會在凌晨出現。沒多久，他聽到時鐘敲響報時一點鐘。

「沒事！沒有人在這裡！」他想，「這一切不過是一場惡夢罷了。」

就在他慶幸一切都沒事之際，一陣光芒忽然布滿整個房間，他看到一個白色的身影就站在床腳。那人的臉看起來很年輕，穿著一身雪白的衣服。

「你……你就是第一個幽靈？」施顧己問。

「沒錯，我就是。」幽靈平靜地回答，「我是過去的聖誕節幽靈。」

「誰的過去？」

「你的過去。」幽靈引他來到窗邊，接著將他帶出窗外。

p. 46–47 一轉眼他們已經站在鄉間，時序正值美麗的冬日。

「這是……這是我出生的地方。」施顧己喊道。接著他憶起孩童時代的歡樂。

「你很傷心嗎？」幽靈問他。

「不，我很……開心。」施顧己說。

「那你為什麼要哭呢？」

「我沒有哭。」施顧己回答，不過他能感到自己臉頰上的淚水。

施顧己和幽靈慢步走向小村莊，他們走近了些，就聽到遠處孩子們玩耍的嬉戲聲。孩子們剛從一間小學校放學回來，因為放假了，他們高興得又叫又笑。

「他們並不是真實的。」過去的聖誕幽靈說，「他們只不過是過去聖誕節所留下的靈魂，他們也看不見你和我。」

但是施顧己認識這些靈魂，就像他認識這裡的街道、房舍和居民一樣。

p. 48–49 「來吧！」幽靈説，「還有一個孩子被獨自留在學校。」

「我知道，」施顧己難過地説，「我知道。」幽靈看到施顧己的眼中泛著淚光。

現在學校裡又冷又暗，一個小男孩坐在書桌前看書，施顧己在小男孩的隔壁桌子坐下，哭了起來。

「這……這是我。」施顧己説，「我小時候曾經被留在這裡過聖誕節，我的父母親都不在家。現在我真希望我當時……」施顧己忽然沈默起來。

「什麼？你希望什麼？」幽靈禮貌地問他。

「沒什麼，現在是來不及了。」施顧己沈重地説，「昨天晚上，有個小男孩到我辦公室窗前為我唱聖誕歌曲，結果我什麼也沒有給他，還氣呼呼地叫他滾開。現在我倒希望那時我有給他一些東西……」

幽靈微笑道：「現在該去看另一個聖誕節了。」

p. 50–51 他們又回到學校，這一次小施顧己長大了一些，學校看起來比之前更老舊、更黯淡，唯一不變的是，只有施顧己一個人坐在書桌前。

這時教室的門被打開，一個小女孩跑進來。

「艾伯納瑟，是我，你妹妹法蘭。」小女孩説著跑到施顧己面前，抱著他，「爸爸現在已經變好了，他改變了主意，要你回家。」

「我可以回家了？」小施顧己驚訝地問，「爸爸要我回家？」

當老施顧己看到這一幕，又一滴眼淚從臉頰滑下，那一年的聖誕節真的是很快樂。

「我妹妹法蘭是個好女人。」施顧己説，「她老是很開心，對每個人都很好。」

「她有生下一個孩子，是吧？」幽靈問，「在她過世之前？」

「沒錯，幽靈，就是我外甥佛瑞德，他和我妹妹一樣，性格很樂天、很善良。」他想起白天稍早見到佛瑞德的情景，想起自己拒絕他的晚餐邀約，這讓他心情更沈重。

p. 52–53 現在幽靈帶施顧己來到一個繁忙、擁擠的城市，他們直接走向一間辦公室。

「你還記得這裡嗎？」聖誕幽靈問他。

「當然，」施顧己開心地大叫，「這裡是老費茲威先生的辦公室，我第一個工作的地方，費茲威先生是個快樂善良的老闆。」

幽靈和施顧己走進辦公室，一個心寬體胖的男人坐在辦公桌前工作，這時他突然把兩名員工叫過來。「迪克，艾伯納瑟，」他高喊著，「今天可是聖誕夜啊，該放下工作，好好慶祝一下！」

迪克和施顧己興奮地放下手中的帳簿和文件，開始生火。

「我記得迪克，」老施顧己説，「他曾是我最好的朋友。」

就在這時，費茲威太太和三個女兒走進辦公室，他們身後還跟著更多的年輕人。大家都在和朋友談天，隨著音樂起舞，享用豐盛的食物。

p. 54–55 施顧己陶醉地看著這場聖誕舞會。「過去的我和現在很不一樣。」他默默想著。

「大家都喜歡費茲威先生，」聖誕幽靈説，「為什麼啊？這場舞會看起來一點也不怎麼樣，説不定大家都太傻了，為了一點小事就高興成這樣。」

「不是這樣子的，幽靈！你錯了！」施顧己說。「費茲威先生是我們的老闆，我們快不快樂，都是掌握在他手中的，他可以讓我們的工作輕鬆愉快，也可以讓我們做得很痛苦。這場舞會對我們而言很特別，它帶給我們歡樂，甚至比金錢報酬更有意義。」施顧己訝異自己會說出這些話。

「你在想些什麼？」幽靈問，看得出施顧己被事情困擾著。

「我想到我的職員，鮑伯‧克來契。」施顧己回答。

「來吧，時間不多了。」幽靈說，「我們還有另一個聖誕節要看。」

p. 56–57 場景再度變換，施顧己看見一名四十歲的男人，那是他自己。現在他看得很清楚，時間會改變一個人，他如今顯然已經變得對錢非常的重視。

「善良的幽靈，求求你，我不想再看了。」施顧己喊道，因為他記起了當時的情景。

施顧己和一名年輕女孩並肩坐著，女孩原本是他的未婚妻，而她正在哭泣。

「不，太遲了，」她說，「現在你已經有了另一個愛人了。」

「什麼？什麼另一個愛人？」施顧己問。

「就是錢呀！」女孩回答，「現在的你只愛錢，並不愛我。我們剛認識時，我相信你是愛我的，但那份愛現在已經不在了。因為我沒有錢，你就不再愛我了。再見了！祝你有那些錢能過得愉快！」

「我求你，幽靈，不要再看了，我想要回家了。」施顧己痛苦悔恨地吼著。

「不，施顧己，」幽靈說，「還有一個聖誕節，快一點吧，時間不多了。」

p. 58–59 上一個場景後又過了數年，在房間裡，一個漂亮的小女孩和母親一起站在爐火邊，這母親就是施顧己前未婚妻，她正看著孩子們開心地玩耍。

就在此時，父親進門了，懷裡抱著滿滿的聖誕禮物，他將禮物一個個發給孩子。拆禮物時他們開心地笑著叫著。

他們感謝父母親送給的禮物，接著孩子們便回房睡覺了。現在整個房間都安靜下來，只剩下那個男人與妻子。

丈夫對她說：「今天我見到妳的老朋友，艾伯納瑟・施顧己，我路過他的辦公室，他們說馬里已經病危了。可憐的施顧己，要是馬里走了，他在世上就一個朋友也沒有了。」

「幽靈！不要再看了！求求你！」施顧己吼道，「我不想再看下去了。」

「這就是你的人生，」幽靈說，「這些都是你過去的聖誕節，你一直以來是如何過日子的，艾伯納瑟・施顧己？」幽靈問，「這些事都已經發生，再也無法改變了，只有未來能改變。」

接著幽靈便消失了。施顧己回到自己床上，心刺痛著。

p. 62–63

［第四章］現在的聖誕幽靈

施顧己醒過來，坐在床上。他聽見教堂的鐘聲，時間又是凌晨一點——第二個聖誕幽靈出現的時刻到了。

從門下的縫隙間，施顧己看到一陣強光從隔壁房間冒出。他慢慢地走到門口，把門打開。

在房間的中央，一個幽靈就坐在沙發上。他身材高大肥胖，臉上掛著歡樂的笑容，他看起來和前一個聖誕幽靈很不一樣。

「我是現在的聖誕幽靈，」幽靈開口說道，「今晚你要跟著我，從我帶你看的一切情景中學習。」

「好的，」施顧己說，「我想要學，昨晚的幽靈帶我看了很多，現在我還想要看更多。」

幽靈抓住施顧己的手，便一起消失了。

p. 64–65 下一秒他們就出現在職員鮑伯・克來契的家中。克來契太太和女兒們正在擺設聖誕晚餐的餐桌，當陣陣香味瀰漫在狹小乾淨的屋裡，大伙都感到興奮又開心。

這時鮑伯帶著最小的兒子小提姆從教堂回來。小提姆是個非常特別的小男孩，以他的年紀來看，他長得特別矮小，而且如果不用枴杖就無法走路。

「大家聖誕快樂！」鮑伯說，「這是什麼香味啊？」

「那是聖誕烤鵝啊，爸爸！」孩子們喊著。他們沒有人說那隻鵝對這一大家子人來說似乎太小了。

施顧己和聖誕幽靈看著這家人坐在餐桌前，雖然那是一桌非常簡單的聖誕大餐，但一家人仍和樂融融。

餐後全家人圍聚在爐火旁，小提姆坐得很靠近爐火，他病得很重。

p. 66–67 「麻煩你，幽靈，告訴我，」施顧己問，「小提姆會活下來嗎？」

「未來是可以改變的，」幽靈說，「但此刻在小提姆的座位上，我只看見一張空椅子。」聽到這些話施顧己一臉難過。

「但你幹嘛在乎？」幽靈問，「你不是說過世上的人已經太多了嗎？小提姆要是死了，對你來說不是件好事嗎？」

施顧己想起自己在辦公室對那兩名紳士說過的話，不由得心生慚愧。

　　就在這時，他聽到了鮑伯提到他的名字。

　　「我們為施顧己先生乾一杯吧！」鮑伯說。

　　「為施顧己？」他太太氣憤地說，「我們為什麼要為那個老吝嗇鬼乾杯？」

　　「因為今天是聖誕節啊！」鮑伯回答。

　　「好吧，你是對的，」他太太回答，「但是不管我們做什麼，那個壞老頭都不會感到開心的。」

　　`p. 68` 幽靈帶著他來到街上，他們所到之處，都聽到人們對彼此快樂地高喊聖誕快樂。沒多久，他們又來到他所認識的另一個家庭。

　　他和幽靈走進明亮、溫暖的房間，這家人都坐在那兒。大伙聽著他外甥說故事，聽得哈哈大笑。

　　「所以，當我對施顧己舅舅說『聖誕快樂』之後，他只說了一句：『呸！騙人的玩意兒！』」佛瑞德談到他去施顧己辦公室的情形。

　　「我想他應該是相信聖誕節的，」施顧己的外甥說，「你能想像嗎？聖誕節是騙人的玩意兒？」

　　「我從來都不喜歡那個刻薄的老頭，」佛瑞德太太說道，「他那麼有錢，卻從不幫助別人，甚至連自己也都過著像窮人一般的生活。」

　　`p. 70–71` 接著他們開始玩遊戲，遊戲名稱叫做「20 個問題」，每個人都要想出一樣東西，由其他人提出問題，來猜出那樣東西是什麼。

　　輪到佛瑞德的時候，每個人都對他提出問題。

「是一種動物嗎？」有個客人問。

「是的。」施顧己的外甥回答。

「住在城市裡嗎？」另一個人問。

「沒錯。」施顧己的外甥又回答。

其他客人問的問題，讓大家得知這種動物不是狗啊貓啊之類，也不是會被拿來食用的動物，而且這種動物會說話。

終於，輪到佛瑞德的太太發問了。

「有人喜歡它嗎？」她問。

「沒有。」施顧己的外甥悲哀地說。

「我知道是什麼了。」他太太回答。

「如果是一種沒有人會喜歡的動物，那一定就是你的舅舅施顧己了！」她答對了！

「不過我還是祝老先生聖誕快樂，也祝新年快樂。」佛瑞德說，覺得這真不是個太好的遊戲。

施顧己想要說「聖誕快樂」，但眼前的景象旋即消失。

p. 72–73 就在幽靈將他帶走之際，施顧己看了幽靈一眼。幽靈的外貌不再年輕，現在看起來已經老了。

「你的生命是不是很短暫？」施顧己問幽靈。

「是的，非常短，」幽靈回答，「我只能活到聖誕節的午夜，我的時間不多了，不過在我死之前想讓你再看一幕。」

幽靈指著兩個小孩，他們十分瘦弱，在寒冷的天氣中不斷發抖。施顧己望向他們的眼睛，看得出來他們又難過又飢餓，而且已經餓得不成人形了。

「他們沒有父母，」幽靈說道，「沒有食物，沒有家人，沒有錢上學。他們一無所知，一無所有，而他們會永遠一無所知，一無所有。」

「沒有人幫助他們嗎？」施顧己喊道。

「不是有孤兒院嗎？」幽靈反問，「唉，別人有什麼義務要幫助他們呢？這世界上的人已經那麼多……」

就在這時，教堂鐘聲敲了十二下，施顧己四處尋找幽靈，但它已經失去蹤影了。

p. 76~77 狄更斯時代的倫敦

在施顧己生活的那個年代，工業革命為倫敦所帶來的苦難愈演愈烈。工廠林立，人們工作一整天卻只能領取微薄的薪水，也是司空見慣的事。許多家庭人口眾多，甚至一個家庭就有十幾個孩子！

對窮人來說，這真是一個慘澹的年代。過於擁擠的人口使得污染問題更加嚴重，走在街道上，都可以聞到垃圾的惡臭，而且也沒有乾淨的水可飲用或烹煮。諸等情況助長疾病迅速蔓延，造成大量的人口死亡。

由於大部分家庭的成員眾多且窮困，兒童每天在工廠工作超過十六小時的情形非常普遍。很多人舉債度日，但根本無力償還借款，因此鋃鐺入獄。

p. 78~79

[第五章] 未來的聖誕幽靈

施顧己看到下一位聖誕幽靈來到他面前，但是和另外兩名幽靈不太一樣的是，施顧己看不到這個幽靈的臉和身體，只看得出這個幽靈很高，他穿著黑色的長袍，戴著黑色的兜帽。

「你是未來的聖誕幽靈嗎？」施顧問道，聲音些微顫抖著。

幽靈沒有作聲，只是從衣服裡伸出一隻修長蒼白的手，打個手勢示意沒錯。

「你會帶我去看未來嗎？」施顧己問。

這次幽靈還是沒回答，只是走了起來。

沒多久，他們便來到城中央。他們來到的第一個地方，是生意人常去的場所。人們會穿著昂貴的西裝，把手插在口袋裡，四處走動，施顧己還可以聽到一些人在說話。

「就我所知，」一名肥胖商人說，「他正是在聖誕夜去世的。」

「那他的錢怎麼處理？」一個人問道。

「沒人知道，」另一個人回答，「不過可以確定的是，他的喪禮會很簡陋，根本沒有人喜歡他。」

p. 80–81 「他們是在說誰啊？」施顧己問。

幽靈沒有回答，逕自帶著施顧己來到城裡比較貧窮的另一區。這裡的街道擁擠、狹窄而骯髒，與剛才看過的那些穿著體面的生意人比起來，這裡的人是非常不一樣的。

他們走進其中一間狹小、污穢的商店，店裡賣的都是些舊東西，舊衣服、舊鑰匙、舊絞練和舊碗盤。

施顧己突然明白這是人們缺錢時會來的當鋪。

店鋪的老闆，喬，坐在髒兮兮的桌子後面抽著菸。

一名老婦人站在他面前，手裡緊握著一個大盒子。

「給我一些錢吧，喬，我這次給你帶來了一些好東西。」

喬打開盒子往裡面看。「床罩？」喬驚訝地提高音量。「是從他的床上拿下來的？他死的那張床上？」

「當然，為什麼不拿，他又用不到了。」老婦人回答，「我還拿了他喪禮時所穿的那件昂貴襯衫。」

p. 82–84 就在這時，另一個女人拿著更多東西走進店裡，她過去是那位老人的管家。

「快過來，喬，看看我袋子裡的東西，告訴我這些東西可以換多少錢。」管家貪婪地問道。

喬仔細地檢查了每一件物品，最後他拿出兩張紙，寫下一些數字，再把紙交給兩位婦女，對她們說：「這是我出的價錢，我只會給這麼多，再多就沒有了。」

那些錢是不多，但是比起她們為老闆賣力工作所得的工資，這價錢是多得多了。

「真可笑，」喬說道，「那老頭這麼努力工作了一輩子就是為了錢，到頭來享受利益的卻是我們！」兩個女人回了一個殘酷的冷笑。

p. 84–85 突然間，場景變換了，施顧己站在一張沒有床罩被單的床鋪面前。床上只有一層薄薄的床單，施顧己看到床單覆蓋的是一具屍體，幽靈指示施顧己去看看屍體的臉。

「不，幽靈，我不能看，」施顧己說，聲音因恐懼而顫抖。

「這太傷感了，這老人孤獨地死去，沒有人愛他，沒有人懷念他。過去他不關心人，只關心錢。我會永遠忘不了這一幕，實在太慘了，我們現在可以離開了嗎？」

場景再度改變，現在他們來到鮑伯‧克來契的家，施顧己看到鮑伯走進來。鮑伯的外表看起來變老了，臉色顯得非常疲憊，這次小提姆並沒有跟在他身邊，全家人來到他面前，而他哭了起來。

「我好想念我的孩子，想再見見我的孩子。」他哭喊著。

鮑伯走到樓上小提姆的房間，房裡空蕩蕩的。那天稍早小提姆離開人世了，就在聖誕節這一天。施顧己感覺到眼淚從臉頰落下。

p. 86–87 現在他們回到城裡的大街上，但施顧己一直無法忘懷那老人的死，還是想知道那到底是誰。

「拜託你告訴我那個死去的人到底是誰。」施顧己懇求幽靈，幽靈只是靜靜看著他，然後繼續往前走。幽靈突然在墓園停下，直接領他走向其中一個墳墓。

施顧己的頭顫抖著，他抬起眼，唸出墓碑上的名字──**艾伯納瑟·施顧己**。

施顧己跌坐在地上，「不！不！不可能！」

他大喊著，「我發誓我會改，快跟我說還是有希望的，所以你才要來帶我看這些的，不是嗎？」

幽靈一句話也沒説。

「我以後會慶祝聖誕節！我會幫助別人！求求你，幽靈，告訴我我的未來是可以改變的。」

但是幽靈已經離開了，施顧己也已回到家中，蓋著毯子躺在床上。

p. 90

[第六章] 聖誕快樂！

「我還有時間！」施顧己高喊，「我還有時間改變我的生活！謝謝你們，三個幽靈，我永遠不會忘記你們為我上的這一課！也謝謝你，雅各·馬里，你一直都是我的好朋友！」

施顧己很慶幸自己依然活著，更高興還有時間來改變自己的未來。

「首先我可以做什麼？」他想，「我可以先幫助誰？」

他打開窗戶，窗外的天空明亮，陽光普照，他看到一個小男孩獨自走在樓下的人行道上。

「請問你，年輕人，今天是幾月幾號？」施顧己問那個小男孩，小男孩一臉驚訝。

「今天是聖誕節，先生。」小男孩回答。

p. 92–93 「聖誕節！」施顧己很訝異，三個幽靈帶他去了那麼多地方卻只花了一晚。

他把小男孩叫住，「年輕人，你知道街上那位屠夫的店嗎？」

「當然知道。」男孩回答。

「那好」，施顧己說，「櫥窗裡展示的那隻肥鵝，你知道被賣出去了沒有？」

「那隻鵝？和我差不多大的那隻？」男孩回道，「我知道還沒有賣出去。」

「太好了，」施顧己說，「麻煩你去跟屠夫說我要買，如果你快點回來，我就給你很好的小費。」

「我要把那隻鵝送到克來契家。」他想。

沒多久屠夫和小男孩就來到施顧己家門前，屠夫捧著那隻大肥鵝，施顧己給了小男孩不少小費，還祝他「聖誕快樂」！接著他付錢買下那隻鵝，還付了計程車費送到克來契家，又給了屠夫一些小費。

p. 94–95 施顧己穿上他最好的衣服走上街，臉上掛著微笑，顯得很開心。人們看到這麼一位愉悅的紳士，都對他說：「早！聖誕快樂！」施顧己也一一打招呼回去。

終於，他找到了他要找的人──昨天的那兩位紳士。

「不好意思，先生，你們記得我嗎？」施顧己問，「昨天你們來過我的辦公室，要募款幫助窮人。」

「喔，對了，」其中一人說，「是施顧己先生嗎？」

「是的，沒錯。昨天的事我很抱歉，」施顧己說，「我只是想道個歉，還有……」接著施顧己把臉湊到他耳邊低語。

「真的嗎？」那個男人不敢置信，「您真是非常慷慨！有了那筆錢，我們可以幫助很多很多人。」

「好，明天就請來我辦公室一趟，我會把錢交給你。」施顧己說，「還有，祝你們聖誕快樂！」接著他便繼續往前走。

p. 96–97 他繼續往前走，那天下午，他來到外甥家門前。

敲門的時候，他很緊張。他昨天很無禮，要是外甥為此在氣頭上，那該怎麼辦？如果外甥媳不願意讓他進門，又該如何呢？

終於，一個小女孩把門打開。

「哈囉！聖誕快樂！」施顧己說，「我可以進來嗎？我是妳爸爸的朋友。」小女孩讓他進門，還帶他來到餐廳，所有人都圍坐在餐桌前，桌上擺著豐盛的聖誕大餐。

「各位，聖誕快樂！」施顧己走進來說道。

「呃，哈囉，也祝您聖誕快樂。」佛瑞德滿臉詫異地答道，「謝謝您來加入我們。」

施顧己坐下，享受了這輩子最快樂的一次聖誕節。這個和善、親切、煥然一新的施顧己，和每個人都相談甚歡。

在他要離開時，他們都感謝他的參加，還祝他「新年快樂」！

p. 98-99 第二天，施顧己一大早就來到辦公室，他在等職員鮑伯‧克來契，然而鮑伯並沒有一早就到公司。最後鮑伯晚了十五分鐘才進辦公室，這種情況一向會讓施顧己大為光火。鮑伯趕緊走到辦公桌前，開始做起事來。

但今天不同於往常，施顧己並沒有生氣。

「你的聖誕節過得快樂嗎，鮑伯？」施顧己問。

鮑伯抬起頭，一臉驚訝，他本來以為施顧己會說些刻薄話。

「是的，老闆，我過得很快樂。」鮑伯回答，「有個善心人送來一隻大肥鵝給我們做聖誕晚餐，這是我家人這麼久以來吃到最好的一餐。」

聽到這裡，施顧己很歡喜，但是他並沒有告訴鮑伯鵝是他送的，這是他心裡的小秘密。

「那真是太好了，鮑伯。」施顧己說，「我也有個消息要告訴你。」

這讓鮑伯感到非常緊張。

「從今天開始，你會的薪水會調漲，才能好好照料你一家人。」施顧己微笑說著。接著，他生了大大的爐火，讓他們可以在溫暖的地方工作。

小提姆並沒有死，施顧己成了他們家的另一位父親，而且從此之後，他再也沒說過「騙人的玩意」這字了。

Answers

P. 26   **(A)** miserly, cold, mean

  (B) **1** - (c)   **2** - (b)   **3** - (a)

  (C) **1** - (b)   **2** - (a)   **3** - (c)

P. 27   **(D)** **1** (b)   **2** (a)

  (E) **1** F   **2** F   **3** T   **4** T

P. 40   **(A)** **3** → **4** → **2** → **5** → **1**

  (B) **1** cost   **2** lit   **3** shook   **4** wore   **5** froze

P. 41   **(C)** **1** cannot   **2** must   **3** cannot

  (D) **1** (b)   **2** (c)

P. 60   **(A)** **1** T   **2** T   **3** F   **4** F   **5** F

  (B) **1** on   **2** with   **3** for   **4** of

P. 61   **(C)** **1** - (a)   **2** - (c)   **3** - (b)

  (D) **1** (b)   **2** (a)   **3** (a)

P. 74   **(A)** **1** - (d)   **2** - (c)   **3** - (b)   **4** - (a)   **5** - (e)

  (B) **1** F   **2** F   **3** T   **4** F   **5** T

P. 75   **(C)** **1** couch   **2** crutch   **3** goose
  4 miser   **5** monsters

  (D) **1** Or   **2** time

P. 88   **A**   **1** T   **2** F   **3** T   **4** F

      B   **1** (c)   **2** (b)

P. 89   **C**   **1** signaled   **2** walked   **3** holding
              4 looked   **5** miss

      D   **1** with her hands in her pockets
            2 with their eyes closed

P. 100   **A**   **5** → **1** → **4** → **3** → **2**

       B   **1** - ⓒ   **2** - ⓐ   **3** - ⓑ   **4** - ⓔ   **5** - ⓓ

P. 114   **A**   **1** selfish   **2** goose   **3** butcher   **4** nephew

       B   **1** At the end of the story Scrooge believes in ghosts. (T)
            2 Scrooge didn't like his sister, Fran, very much. (F)

P. 115   **C**   **1** What did Scrooge say about Christmas at first? (c)
            2 Why did Bob want to drink to Scrooge? (a)
            3 Why did Fred always invite his uncle Scrooge to Christmas dinner? (a)

       D   **1** Scrooge didn't like Christmas.
            2 Scrooge saw the Ghost of Christmas Present.
            3 Scrooge saw himself as a young boy at school.
            4 Scrooge saw his name on the grave.
            5 Scrooge donated money to the poor, and a goose to Bob's family.

               < **1** → **3** → **2** → **4** → **5** >

小氣財神【二版】
A Christmas Carol

作者 _ 查爾斯・狄更斯
　　　（Charles Dickens）
改寫 _ Scott Fisher
插圖 _ Ludmila Pipchenko
翻譯 / 編輯 _ 羅竹君
作者 / 故事簡介翻譯 _ 王采翎
校對 _ 王采翎
封面設計 _ 林書玉
排版 _ 葳豐／林書玉
播音員 _ Amy Lewis, Michael Yancey
製程管理 _ 洪巧玲
發行人 _ 周均亮
出版者 _ 寂天文化事業股份有限公司
電話 _ +886-2-2365-9739
傳真 _ +886-2-2365-9835
網址 _ www.icosmos.com.tw
讀者服務 _ onlineservice@icosmos.com.tw
出版日期 _ 2019年12月 二版一刷（250201）
郵撥帳號 _ 1998620-0 寂天文化事業股份有限公司

Adaptor of **A Christmas Carol**

Scott Fisher

Michigan State University
(Asian Studies)
Seoul National University
(MA, Korean Studies)
Ewha Womans University, Graduate
School of Translation and
Interpretation, English Professor

國家圖書館出版品預行編目資料

　　小氣財神 / Charles Dickens 原著；Scott Fisher
改寫 . -- 二版 . -- [臺北市]：寂天文化, 2019.12
　　　面； 公分 . -- (Grade 3 經典文學讀本)
　　譯自：A Christmas carol
　　ISBN 978-986-318-866-7(25K 平裝附光碟片)

1. 英語　　2. 讀本

805.18　　　　　　　　　　　　　　108019938